Unsung Melodies

Unsung Melodies

by

Angela K Parker

Unsung Melodies
Copyright © 2022 by Angela K. Parker
All Rights Reserved.

Without limiting the rights under copyright reserved above, no part of this publication may be reproduced, stored in or introduced into a retrieval system, or transmitted, in any form, or by any means electronic, mechanical, photocopying, recording, or otherwise, without the prior written permission of the author of this book.

This novel is a work of fiction. Names, characters, businesses, places, events, and incidents are either the products of the author's imagination or used in a fictitious manner. Any resemblance to actual persons, living or dead, or actual events is purely coincidental.

Published: Angela K. Parker 2022
angelaparkerauthor@gmail.com

"Cover Design ©Angela K Parker"
ISBN: 9798798037704

Dedication

To living life to the fullest despite the obstacles in our paths

Contents

One	1
Two	10
Three	21
Four	37
Five	52
Six	59
Seven	66
Eight	78
Nine	90
Ten	106
Eleven	113
Twelve	120
Thirteen	127
Fourteen	137
Fifteen	147
Sixteen	156
Seventeen	164
Eighteen	176

Nineteen	*187*
Twenty	*194*
Twenty-One	*197*
Twenty-Two	*210*
Twenty-Three	*224*
Twenty-Four	*232*
Twenty-Five	*242*
Twenty-Six	*252*
Twenty-Seven	*260*
Twenty-Eight	*269*
Epilogue	*278*
Acknowledgments	*286*
Author's Note	*288*
Until Next Time...	*289*
About the Author	*290*
Connect With the Author	*291*

One

Owen

Relationships.

Everyone around me seems to be involved in one. Gone are the days of late nights and one-night stands. I've only had a few, but random flings have lost their appeal over time. I'm the only bachelor in the group now, and it's starting to hit me big time. I've always wanted something more serious. It's just taking me a little longer to find the right fit.

I had an urge once—to shoot my shot and join the majority—but I didn't act on it. How could I, when the woman I desired was my best friend's sister?

I remember the first time I saw Sophia Conley sitting in the front row at Dalton's wedding. She was beautiful in her long black dress. I kept stealing glances at the small piece of thigh visible through the side slit. She had a look of longing on her face, and I couldn't fathom how someone could ever let her go.

I recall thinking how good she'd make me look if she were mine, how she'd be much more than just another woman on my arm. But I decided to keep my thoughts to myself.

Besides the fact that Sophia is Dalton's sister, she also has a child. Her reality was already complicated without adding me to it. And I had no idea if Dalton would go for it. He and Sophia had only recently connected due to their late father wanting to keep her a secret. Since then, Dalton has taken the role of big brother seriously, even though he's only one year older, and despite that, Sophia is a grown woman. He'd likely flip if I even tried to dip my straw in her cup.

A shrill scream pierces the air, and my eyes spring open behind my shades at the sound of Sophia's voice. I sit upright on the lounge chair, my eyes darting in the direction she's pointing.

"Ellis, no!" Sophia yells, with her arms outstretched as if she could somehow stop him. She runs toward the pool, but it's too late.

Tiny legs wilt beneath a small body, hitting the cement by the pool. Ellis lands on his side and quickly sits up, nursing his elbow. He glances at me, seemingly stunned into silence momentarily, until his eyes find his mother. He belts out a harsh cry, and I leap into action. It all happened so fast, and I was next to him in an instant.

I push my shades on my head as I try to assess the damage, but Ellis kicks me away, crying harder, reaching out for Sophia.

Sophia pulls Ellis into her arms the second she's next to him, her eyes frantically worrying over every inch of his body. He has a sizable scrape along his left arm and a smaller one on his left leg, but nothing that would require stitches.

"Are you okay, Baby? Mommy's here," Sophia croons. She glances my way, rocking Ellis in her arms. "Sorry about the kick. He didn't mean it."

"Not a problem," I responded.

I know that her kid is hurt, which should be my focus right now, but I can't help but pause to admire the woman in front of me. How her fingers grazed the skin of my arm as she reached down to scoop Ellis into her arms. It didn't mean anything to her, and I doubt she even felt it, but I did. I noticed, and now I can't stop staring.

Snap out of it, Owen.

I tear my eyes away from Sophia, looking down at Ellis in her arms for a moment. "I can carry him inside for you." I reach for Ellis as my eyes return to Sophia.

"No." She pulls away from me, clutching Ellis tighter. Her eyes close as she sighs. "Sorry." She looks at me. "He's kind of shy," she explains. "I'll take care of him."

"What happened?" Dalton squats next to Sophia, taking control of the situation before I can respond.

"He's fine," Sophia says.

Dalton ignores her, scoops Ellis up, and stands, turning toward his house.

Sophia rolls her eyes and rises, too, giving me a final glance before going after them.

I feel the urge to follow them too but decide against it. I want to know that they are okay. Sophia flinching struck me as odd. She doesn't know me, but she has to know that I would never hurt her. Dalton is like family to me, which makes her family too.

I run my fingers through my hair, staring at them as they pass through the sliding glass door at the rear of Dalton's home. Then I huff out a deep breath and return to my position on the lounge chair.

I probably should've made up an excuse to ditch this party, but it's my nephew's birthday. Daddy Dalton decided to use uncle Luke and uncle Owen as chaperones. Brodie probably won't even remember this. The kid just turned two.

I slip my shades back over my eyes and prop one leg up in the chair, watching the pool. My mind is not all there, though. I can't stop thinking about Sophia and Ellis.

There are only five kids here, and they're all heavily guarded by their parents. I could check on Sophia and Ellis, but Dalton would wonder why.

Or maybe not.

I am a trusted chaperone. I wouldn't be doing my job if I didn't follow up, right?

I stand and make my way inside, unable to resist any longer. I follow the voices to the guest room on the first floor and walk inside. Ellis is sitting on the bathroom counter beside the sink. Sophia is standing next to him, holding his hand.

Dalton throws something into the trash and steps in front of Ellis. "Okay, Champ," he says to Ellis, balling his hand into a fist.

Ellis smiles widely, bumping his fist against Dalton's.

Sophia smiles too, and the whole room shines around her as she does. The corner of my lips twitch, and I quickly reel it in, averting my gaze.

I knock once on the wall outside the bathroom door. "Is he alright?" I ask, nodding toward Ellis.

Dalton looks at me. Sophia glances at my bare chest and swallows deeply before moving her eyes to Ellis.

"He's fine," Dalton says. "Just a bruised ego." He lifts Ellis and walks him to the bed, sitting him down.

Sophia follows, refusing to look at me as she passes.

"Would you mind keeping them company for a few minutes before he goes back out?" Dalton asks me.

I could say no. I should say no, but I can't pass up the opportunity to be near Sophia. "Sure," I drag out, confused and slightly frightened to be alone with her.

"I don't need a babysitter, Dalton," Sophia says, annoyed. I can't tell if her attitude is aimed at him or me. "I'm twenty-five years old, and I'm pretty sure I'm capable of taking care of Ellis on my own. You know, as I've done for the past four and a half years."

"Babysitter's not for you," Dalton responds. "Thanks," he says to me on his way out the door.

Sophia opens her mouth to say more, but it's too late. Dalton's gone, leaving me to decide if I should go too. I don't want to be here if she doesn't want me.

"Ugh," Sophia grunts out, and it's the sweetest sound of frustration that I've ever heard. "Sorry," she turns to me, then sits next to Ellis on the bed. "I love having a brother, but he's so overbearing."

"I know," I responded, amused. "And you don't have to keep apologizing."

"Hmm?" Sophia asks.

"May I?" I gesture to the empty spot next to Ellis.

"Sure," Sophia says, her brows bunched.

I sit, and Ellis squints his eyes at me, moving his body closer to his mom.

"You keep saying you're sorry," I tell Sophia.

"Oh, sor…." Sophia pauses and lets out a laugh. "Just being polite."

"It's not necessary."

Sophia raises an eyebrow. "You'd prefer it if I wasn't?"

"Yes," I blurt out, then realize my mistake. "No. This isn't going the way I'd hoped."

Her brow rises again. "The way you'd hoped?" She questions.

I glance at Ellis, who's still watching me closely. I had no hope when I came inside to find them. I only wanted to be close to her. Now that I am, I don't know what to do or say. My words are definitely not coming out right.

I only know the basics about Sophia through Dalton. She's a single mom. Lives alone. Works as an Estate Planner. And she's beautiful.

Dalton didn't say the latter, but my eyes don't lie. She is gorgeous.

Sophia has a story to tell. I know she does. I'm just not sure if I'm deserving of it. Still, I selfishly want to know everything.

The way she's behaving—her posture and tone—screams, *not available*. There's an unexplainable sadness in her smile. An air of caution in her eyes. Like she's been hurt too many times and doesn't want to be hurt again.

"I just wanted to make sure you were okay. That Ellis was okay," I responded nervously.

"Mom, can I go play?" Ellis asks, looking up at Sophia.

Sophia looks down at Ellis. "Sure, Baby. Thank Owen for checking on you."

Ellis' head tilts toward me, his eyes suspicious as he says, "Thank you."

I admire the kid and how cautious he is, even at a young age. "No problem, Bud."

Sophia smiles with approval and reverts her attention to me. "Guess I'll see you around." They stand, and she lets go of Ellis' hand. He takes off running, and she yells after him. "Slow down!"

The tiny glimpse of chaos should turn me off, but it doesn't. I want in. I've never been afraid of commitment. I was waiting for the right woman to come along. Sophia's got that vibe—like maybe she could be the one. Like she'd be worth the effort.

Sophia moves past me toward the door, and I can't resist the urge to stop her.

"Wait." I grab her elbow lightly between my fingers, and she stops, turning slightly toward me. My fingers tingle at the feel of her warm skin.

Sophia looks down at my hand on her elbow and her lips part, releasing a long breath. Her eyes move to my bare chest again, then up to meet my eyes.

"What are you doing later?" I ask, still holding her elbow.

Sophia pulls her arm from my hold, and I immediately regret my words.

What the fuck, Owen? That's not something you say to a single mom.

I'm not much of a conversationalist. I'm known for giving good advice, for knowing the right things to say when I speak. *That* was not right in any way. It sounded cheap and expectant.

Thinking straight is a task when I'm around Sophia. Apparently, it's even worse when I'm touching her. I shouldn't have stopped her, let alone opened my mouth.

"I should go." Sophia turns away from me. As her feet begin to move, I open my mouth again.

"Sophia," I call after her, but she keeps moving without another glance.

Shit!

I assume Sophia only knows me from the tabloids, and I doubt they paint a pretty picture. I'm no stranger to arm candy, and I'm sure I've been photographed with all of them, but I'm not a bad guy. Though, the words that came out of my mouth would beg to differ.

I may have just ruined my chances with Sophia before we got started. And if she tells big brother….

Shit!

I run my hand over my head, resting my palm at the back of my neck, and stare at the open doorway.

What do I do now?

Two

Owen

I've been kicking myself over what I said to Sophia for the last week. I guess she didn't mention it because my body is still intact. I tried thinking of ways to make it up to her and wondering if I should even attempt it. Every time I talk myself out of it, I end up right back where I started.

Still thinking about her.
Still wanting her.
Still needing to conquer the forbidden.
Then the cycle repeats.
I begin to doubt myself.
And I ridicule.
And think of every reason I'm not worthy.

I've asked myself over and over, *"What would a beautiful, smart, single mom want with a twenty-six-year-old musician living over his parent's garage?"*

Sophia is established. She doesn't have time for games.

The thing is, I don't either, but everything she knows about me says that I do. How do I turn that around? How do I get Sophia to see me for who I truly am?

And my parents, they would never approve. It took years for them to get used to my being a musician. They've learned to tolerate my career choice rather than push me away, but they still don't approve of it.

I knew what was expected of me growing up—the whole suit and tie, respectable profession—but that's never been me. I'm all for family and settling down, but I shouldn't have to give up what I love to have that life. I can have both.

My parents' disappointment is why I spent so much time at Dalton's when I was in town. But things changed after he got married. Now I'm stuck here at my parents' home between tours unless I do something about it. Being this close to them more often makes that choice easier by the day. I'm starting to feel like I need my own place. Like life is closing in on me.

My chest tightens when I walk into the main house to find Mom. My head thumps slightly, preparing for the look of disapproval she's always shown me. Or the look that she often doesn't show me at all. I wish we were closer.

"Mom," I call, walking further inside.

"In here." Mom's voice echoes down the hallway.

I follow it to her room, and she barely glances at me when I enter before returning her attention to the mound of towels on her bed.

"Finally came to visit," Mom says, flicking the towel in her hands and folding it. "How long this time?" She asks.

I've been home for over a week, but I've been avoiding my parents, or rather pretending we weren't occupying the same property. And my parents have given me my space until I am ready. That's the way it's always been. I love them, but sometimes my thoughts get in the way, and it's hard for me to express them.

My parents gave me everything growing up, except for the one thing that I truly wanted. Their unconditional love.

I step beside mom and kiss her cheek, then pull away. I grab a towel and fluff it out, making myself useful.

"Two months," I finally responded. "The guys want to spend some time with their families."

Mom's arms pause mid-air as she glances at me. Then she looks away and clears her throat, continuing her task. "And you? What are you going to do with your time?"

I shrug because I have no clue.

The guys and I agreed to switch up our tour schedule once Dalton got married so we'd be home more often. I don't mind it at all, but I still haven't gotten used to the change.

Dalton and Luke have their families to keep them occupied, and they try to include me, when possible, but I don't like feeling like anyone's third wheel.

"I hadn't thought much about it," I answered truthfully. "The guys and I still have our practice sessions while we're here. Otherwise, I guess I'll hang around here and work on some new music."

Mom's nose twitches at my comment, but she doesn't respond.

"Maybe spend some time with you and dad," I continue.

Mom looks at me again while her hands continue to move. "That'd be nice. We haven't eaten a meal together in years."

"It's a plan then. Set the date and time, and I'll be there. My schedule is free for a bit." I smile.

Mom grabs the stack of towels from the bed and walks toward her bathroom. She returns seconds later, placing her hand on my forehead like she did when I was younger.

"Are you feeling okay, Owen?"

I chuckle.

Her question doesn't surprise me at all. She's right. It has been a long time, and I never request to be in their presence when I'm home.

"I'm fine. I just think it's time we put aside our differences. Start acting like a normal family."

Mom blows out a long breath, her lips pursed and body tense. "Okay," she says after a few seconds.

"Okay," I repeat, pulling her in for an awkward hug. "I'll check in later and more often from now on. But right now, there's something I need to do." I kiss her cheek again, then turn for the door.

I call Frank when I step outside to let him know where I'm going so he can meet me there.

Frank is one of our band's bodyguards. Justin, our manager, insists that we have one of them with us at all times. Frank was assigned to me while we were home. So, Frank and I agreed. He doesn't have to sit outside my home all day and night as long as I call before going out alone.

Justin would kill us if he found out, but I didn't see the point of Frank wasting his time since we have a top-notch security system. I felt bad for the guy. As far as I know, he's single, but I think he deserves some kind of life outside DOL.

We all do, which is why I've decided to go after what I want, even if I'm turned down again.

Even if it gets me killed.

· · · · · ♪ ♩ · · · · ·

Is it better that I showed up empty-handed rather than bring flowers?

Sophia's colleagues are eyeing me as if I've made the wrong choice by even stepping one foot into her building. They're probably wondering why the friend is here to see the sister and not her brother.

It's only been a few seconds since the receptionist notified Sophia. I could just leave while my heart and ego are still intact, but I'm no coward.

I walk over to the tinted half-wall glass window to peer outside, crossing my arms over my chest.

"Owen?"

I turn when I hear my name questionably fall from Sophia's mouth. I drop my arms to my sides, and my eyes travel the length of her unintentionally before finding her eyes. I clear my throat and smile.

"Hi." I pause, looking around the waiting room at the eyes focused on us. "Can we talk? In private?"

Sophia looks around the room, a nervous smile appearing on her face. "Sure. Right this way." She nods her head in the opposite direction and begins walking.

I follow behind her, trying to keep my eyes focused on the back of her head and not the sway of her hips as she walks.

She's wearing my favorite color—charcoal gray—and her dress just barely passes her knees. It's not too snug or too short, or too revealing. Her black heels are an added touch. It's respectably sexy on her.

"Here we are." Sophia enters an office with her name plaque on the door, and I follow her inside. She closes the door after me and offers me the chair in front of her mahogany desk. "Do all of you guys have a thing for popping up in offices?" Sophia's lips quirk at the corner and mine along with her.

"He told you about that, huh?"

That's how Dalton and Joselyn became a thing. He showed up at her job after running into her at a club.

Sophia nods. "So, what are you doing here?" She stops at the side of her desk, staring pensively down at me. One hand is on her hip, and her fingers barely touch the desk with the other.

"It's my turn," I tell her, gazing into the soft blue of her eyes.

"For what?"

"To say I'm sorry." I sit forward in the chair, bracing my elbows on the armrests.

"That's not necessary."

"But it is. I realized my approach may have been a little too forward last week. I want to set things straight so there's no bad tension between us."

The air seems to be still for a moment. Then Sophia clears her throat and stands straight, dropping her hand from her hip. She takes two steps back, moving behind her desk to sit in her chair. She entwines her fingers on top of the desk and stares at me.

"Well, your approach *was* forward." Sophia pauses, her eyes holding mine.

I swallow, preparing for her next words.

"But it wasn't inappropriate. It was actually flattering." A blush stains her cheeks, and I smile, relaxing into her words. "I just have so much going on right now. I don't think I'm ready for someone like you, or anyone else for that matter."

And just like that, she brought me back down a notch.

Sophia didn't strike me as the hot and cold type. It's a reminder of how little I know about her.

"Someone like me?"

"Yeah." Sophia shifts in her chair. "You have a lot going on too. With your music and other stuff." Her eyes continue to hold mine accusingly.

"You're right. My music is a big part of my life, but that doesn't mean I don't have space for more."

"And what about the other stuff?" Sophia asks.

"It's irrelevant."

"And what about my brother?"

I chuckle. Sophia has some valid concerns, but I don't give up easily. I want her regardless of the consequences. When I see something I want, I eventually get it. I've held out long enough.

"We'll deal with him when the time comes." I shrug as if it's not a problem.

Sophia squints her eyes, tilting her head slightly before straightening again. "I won't lie to you, Owen. You're an attractive man, but I don't think we should complicate things between us. I have a child to think about, and if things end badly...." Sophia averts her eyes to the window for a moment, closing them and sighing deeply.

"Sophia," I called her attention back to me. Her back straightens. "I could tell you that I'm a good guy. That I won't hurt you. That I think we'd be good together. But showing you would have a much better effect."

Sophia stares at me, and her gloss-covered lips part, her tongue sliding slowly across them.

"Will you go out with me?" I watch her closely, knowing she won't give in right away. I'm prepared for the rejection in her eyes to reach her lips.

"I think...."

"Sophia," I interrupt. "A wise man once said, *Recognize what's right in front of you before it's too late.*"

"Let me guess." Sophia smiles. "That wise man is you."

I nod. "And I'd be a fool to ignore my advice." I lean back in my chair, further away from her desk so that she doesn't feel intimidated. I don't want to scare her away. "What have you got to lose? It's just one date. Give me a chance, and when it's over, you decide if we're something worth pursuing."

"Owen, I can't."

Sophia's rejection hurt deeper than I thought it would, mostly because I haven't been rejected by a woman since, never. It's never happened. Realizing that makes me want her even more, but I can't be one of those guys. The kind that forces his charm on someone uninvited. The kind that stalks and preys.

If Sophia says she's not ready, then I'll wait until she is.

"I respect that," I tell Sophia after a long quiet moment. I stand, keeping my eyes focused on her. "Sorry I stopped by unannounced. Won't happen again." And I mean every word. The next time, I'll make an appointment because this isn't the last she's seen of me.

Mom always told me that relenting is hard, but sometimes you have to do the hard thing to get where you need to be. I've never found much meaning in her words until now.

I wrap my knuckle on her desk twice, then turn for the door.

"Owen," Sophia calls after me just as my fingers wrap around the door handle.

I stop and face her. "Yeah?"

"Maybe we can start slow. With a phone call." Sophia nips nervously at her bottom lip with her teeth.

Excitement leaps into my throat, and I clear it, remaining cool and collected. I don't do phone calls, but for Sophia, I will. And I have a feeling that isn't the only preference she'll be changing.

"I'd like that."

Sophia's eyes twinkle as I walk toward her, but her stance is still so uncertain. I'm looking forward to the moment when that all changes—when I'm able to be close to her, to touch her without that air of hesitance surrounding her.

"May I?" I motion to the pen and paper on her desk, and she nods, her feet shifting beneath her. I grab the pen and paper, scribbling my number down with a small message: *Use at your own risk.*

I probably shouldn't have, but I needed to break the air. And nothing does a better job of that than a cryptic message. It will definitely make Sophia wonder about me. At the very least, it'll make her smile if I'm lucky.

Sophia reads the message after I hand it to her. She fans the small paper in front of her face once, twice, before jerking her hand down. "You're a risk?"

"Everything and everyone is a risk, Sophia. I'm one of the best risks you'll ever take." I grab her free hand and place the pen into it, then slide my fingers over hers as I pull away. "When you're ready." I wink, and I have no clue where the action came from. It just felt right. Then I turn and walk away.

Three

Owen

I was a gentleman.

Not a perfect one, but a gentleman nonetheless.

This must be what it's like for women when they give men all of the power, the waiting and wondering, periodically checking the phone to see if I missed something since the last time it was checked.

Monday. Tuesday. Wednesday. Thursday.

Yeah, it's been a few days, but I'm still holding out hope. Friday is not over yet.

"Earth to Owen."

I snap my head up at the sound of Dalton's voice.

Dalton, Luke, and I are at Dalton's house in the studio out back practicing for an impromptu gig that Justin booked for tonight. The turnout at Lonzo's was huge in the past, and we haven't played there in a few years. I don't mind it since it's local and familiar.

"Are you with us?" Dalton tries again when I don't respond.

"Where else would I be?"

"You tell me. You zoned out on the last run." Dalton Says.

Did I?

I hadn't even realized it.

If Dalton only knew where my thoughts were these days.

"Just trying to get my head together." *Not a lie at all.*

I've been off my game this past week, and I have Sophia to thank for that. It's not that I'm in love with her because I don't know her. Or that I'm lusting after her because I'm not. Guess I can't forget because I've never been pushed aside like an afterthought. It's an enticing sensation that holds my curiosity, making me want to know why.

"Trouble at home?" Luke asks seriously.

I squeeze my eyes shut, pinching the bridge of my nose as if that will help.

There's trouble brewing, just not at home.

"Nope. In fact, my parents and I took the first step toward progress."

Dalton's eyes widened. "Progress?"

"We had dinner Wednesday night as a family."

"And how'd that go?" Luke eyes me curiously.

Luke is usually a jokester, but not at the moment. No one knows better than he and Dalton how weird my relationship is with my parents. It's a serious topic.

"We ate. Mom talked about how understaffed they are at the hospital. Dad kept her calm by agreeing to everything she said, and I listened like a good son. We're thinking about making family dinner a once per week event." I shrug.

"So, tonight should be a breeze," Dalton says.

"Yep. Can we get back to it?" I strum my guitar with the pick between my fingers, and the sound brings me back to the music.

My head has no space for my parents at the moment. Dinner was nice, but it left me feeling like they were avoiding something. That's how it's always been since I was old enough to remember. The older I got, the more protective they became. I suppose all parents are that way, but something feels off with my parents—the way they try and hold on so tightly.

Dalton nods, placing his hand around the mic in front of him.

Luke taps his drum sticks together, confirming he's ready too.

Two minutes into the song, my phone vibrates on the chair beside me, stealing my attention. The caller ID reads Unknown, but I know that it's Sophia. I can feel it.

Sophia doesn't strike me as the type to play hard to get or go along with that type of behavior.

I know it's now or never.

One call.

My only chance.

I stop playing and grab the phone.

"Hello." I placed my guitar in the spot where my phone just sat and stood. Dalton and Luke stare at me like I've grown a second head or lost the one I have. "Sorry, guys. I've got to take this."

I ignore their intense gazes and walk toward the door. I step outside and close the door behind me, and walk away from the studio.

"Hello," I say again, squinting my eyes against the scorching sun. Summertime in Cane, NC, can be brutal.

"Hi. It's Sophia." She hesitates. "Did I call at a bad time?"

"No. We're just practicing for tonight's show."

"Yeah. Dalton mentioned it the other night. Forgot all about it."

"So, you've talked to him?"

"I did. We talk at least twice per week. Dalton insists on it," she grins. "But don't worry. Your office visit didn't come up."

I breathe a sigh of relief. It's not that I don't want anyone to know. I want to shout to the world about whatever this is, but it's too new. I don't even know what *it* is yet, or if *it* will survive past this phone call.

"Will you be there tonight?" I hold my breath, waiting for Sophia's answer.

"I don't know. I've never seen you guys perform live. Could be fun."

"You should come," I insist.

I want to add that I'd love to see her tonight, but I don't. Even if she did come, we wouldn't be alone. But seeing her would be enough for me. She forgot when Dalton told her. So, if she does show up, I think it's safe to say it will be because I asked her to come.

"Maybe. Dalton did say that I could leave Ellis with the sitter at his house, but I don't know."

"You should take him up on the offer."

There's a long pause on the line before Sophia speaks again. "It has been a long time since I've had me-time. I could hang out with the wives for one night, I guess. Joselyn and Rose have been bugging me to take a break for a while now."

I look back inside the studio through the front window, and two sets of eyes are focused on me. I turn away from them. I'm not sure how I'm going to explain this.

"Dalton and Luke are staring me down. I should probably go."

"Yes. Go. I'm sorry for interrupting."

"There you go again apologizing," I chuckle, and Sophia grins through the phone. "If I don't see you tonight, can I call you sometime?"

"You have my number now, so, yes."

Strangely, I don't want to end the call. I want to hear Sophia's voice a little while longer.

"Guess we'll talk later," Sophia says, breaking through my thoughts.

"We will," I answered.

Sophia hangs up, and I take a deep breath before turning toward the studio again. The eyes aren't there anymore, and I hope they won't ask any questions when I get inside.

"What the hell was that?" Luke tilts his head in question as soon as I step through the door.

Well, that didn't pan out as I wanted.

I look from Luke to Dalton and back to Luke, scrounging for an explanation. With everything happening in our family lives, we made a pact that we wouldn't tell lies in this group, and we wouldn't keep secrets.

"Sorry. I'm working on some personal stuff. Planning for my future. Don't have all the details yet, but as soon as it's ironed out, you'll be the first to know." I smile and take my position on the chair, picking up my guitar to get back to work.

It's not technically a secret if there's nothing there yet. I'll just think of it as a surprise.

Dalton squints his eyes at me, then straightens. "Let's run through the set one more time. No interruptions," he says pointedly.

I nod.

I deserve a pass.

I've never walked out on practice. Never missed a show.

I've dealt with their drama over the years without complaint.

I've encouraged them to go after what they want.

Now it's my turn, for whatever happens.

• • • • • ♪ ♪ • • • • •

The crowd goes wild when we take the stage.

I stop at the right of the stage in the background. Spotlights beam down on us from every angle. Faux smoke wisps at our feet.

I jerk my hips from side to side while teasing a chord from the first song.

Our fans' screams seem to get louder. I revel in it, soaking up their energy coursing through my veins like fire.

Dalton looks over, signaling to me, then to the fans, that it's time.

I hold the last note, ending it sharply.

The fans quiet down almost to a hush, and I turn my head in their direction.

Dalton begins by singing acapella. Then Luke and I join in.

The noise comes back full force, and I embrace the zone, falling into the routine I'm used to.

I've always loved what I do. Always felt every melody, every note bone-deep. Tonight, is no different.

We perform for one hour before we exit the stage to freshen up in the dressing room backstage.

Things have changed since the last time we were here. We still have to sign autographs after every show, but it's now done while we're in VIP. No more backstage, up close, and personal private dressing room visits.

There's a long line waiting for us when we get to VIP. The tables around the wall upstairs are occupied now that the show is over. The music is pumping in the background. The bodies not in line are either dancing or standing around talking.

After we're done with autographs, we remain in VIP, just us three and our bodyguards.

I look toward the bar at the front of the club where the wives usually are to see if Sophia came with them. I spot Joselyn and Rose, but Sophia isn't there.

Rose lifts her arm, signaling to someone behind Joselyn. I turn my head in that direction and spot Sophia with her hand in the air in a backward wave.

She came.

She's here because I asked her to come.

My ego swells at the thought.

I place my right elbow on the armrest of the chair with two fingers lightly pressed against my temple. I attempt to be discreet by moving only my eyes while watching Sophia skirt around the crowd. She stays close to the wall, trying not to be noticed. All I can see is her head and glimpses of her face through the crowd as she moves, but I notice.

Sophia looks in my direction, our eyes meeting for a second before she turns away. She stops at the door leading backstage, holding up a badge. The security guard nods and opens the door. Then she disappears from my sight.

I want to go after her.

I look at Dalton and Luke. Both sets of eyes are fixed on the bar where their wives sit chatting with Al, the bartender.

Now is my chance to getaway.

I lean to my right where Luke sits. "I'll be back."

Luke looks at me, a curious smile creeping onto his face. "Business or pleasure?" He asks.

I shrug. "Not sure yet."

"Well, good luck," Luke responds.

I stand, letting Frank know where I'm going, and he motions to club security. Then we walk down a few steps before I'm level with everyone else. I follow one of the club's security guards as he parts the crowd before us. Frank stays close behind me. A few hands reach out to touch me as I pass, and I ignore them.

I've never been keen on the reality of being touched by random strangers without my permission, but it's something I had to get used to in this business. Rules are in place, but some of our fans still think they're entitled to do and say what they want.

I'm really not feeling it tonight. There's only one person on my mind. One set of hands that I'd willingly welcome.

I'm relieved when we reach the door leading backstage, even more so once it's closed behind me.

There's only one place Sophia would've gone.

My eyes hone in on the light shining beneath our dressing room door, and I walk in that direction. I reach for the knob, pausing to speak to Frank.

"Would you mind waiting out here?" I ask.

"Sure," Frank replies with a crook of a smile that quickly vanishes.

Frank rarely smiles. So, I wonder if he knows what I'm up to. He's one of the best at what he does. Trained to notice the smallest things. Hire to keep me safe. He knows the layout of every venue and who is coming and going before I enter. If he agrees with me, he knows Sophia is the only one inside. He must have spoken to the guard at the entrance.

That alone should make me turn around, but Frank is cool. He didn't blab about my visit to Sophia's office. So, I doubt if he'll spill the beans about this without me knowing. My surprise is safe with him. I'm just glad Dalton doesn't read tabloids.

A look of understanding passes between us before I walk inside and close the door behind me.

The room is empty, but I hear the sound of water running behind the bathroom door. I stuff my hands into my pockets, walking further inside. I stop and lean my right shoulder against the wall outside the bathroom door.

The water shuts off, and a beautiful hum replaces the sound. I wonder if Sophia sings too. The door swings open a moment later, and Sophia steps out. She does a double-take in my direction, and on the next step, she freezes. Her mouth opens wide, and she screams at the top of her lungs. Her arms lifted into the air beside her head, her hands shockingly still, and her eyes widened.

"Sophia. Soph, it's me. Owen." I pull my hands from my pockets, cautiously touching the sides of her arms. "It's Owen," I tried again.

Sophia quiets, blinking rapidly with labored breath.

The door to the dressing room swings open. Frank quickly surveys the room from where he stands. Then his gaze falls on me. He looks conflicted and confused.

Maybe my surprise isn't safe with him.

Sophia finally turns to look at him.

"Everything alright, Miss Conley?" Frank asks, moving his eyes over every inch of her.

"Fine." Sophia clears her throat. "I'm fine."

Frank holds her gaze for a few moments. "I'm right outside if you need anything." He gives me a final glance before leaving.

I'm not angry at Frank's reaction at all. We hired our bodyguards to protect us and everyone we value. Sophia falls into that category. She's family, hopefully, one day, in more ways than one. I wouldn't have expected anything less from Frank.

Sophia's eyes close as she blows out a calming breath. When she opens her eyes, she just stares at me, and I stare back.

I can't believe I'm this close to her.

I rub my hands soothingly down her arms.

"I didn't mean to frighten you. I should've announced myself."

Sophia continues to gaze into my eyes, and I still feel a sense of fear from her, but I don't know why.

"I'm glad you came," I told her.

"I was too, but I'm starting to regret my decision. You scared me half to death." Sophia looks down at my hand on her left arm, then up at me.

"Sorry, I didn't want you to panic and start throwing punches." I hold my palms out in surrender.

I hadn't noticed I was still touching her because her bare skin felt so good beneath my fingertips.

I take a moment to look at Sophia. She's even more beautiful than the last time I saw her. Her cheeks are blush pink, her lashes thick, and her lips perfectly glossed. She's wearing black jeans with a short-sleeved teal blouse tucked into the waist, black sneakers, no socks, and her hair is in a single braid down to the center of her back.

Of the few times I've seen Sophia, this is my favorite. There are no wedding, work, or pool party distractions. It's just her and me in an empty room.

"You did warn me that it would be risky," Sophia says with a hint of a smile. "Wise man."

I crack a smile. "You dress down nicely," I say, allowing my eyes to roam over Sophia again.

"Thanks. You're not too shabby either," Sophia says, pinching the arm of my shirt.

The action catches both of us off guard. Sophia quickly drops her hand, and I freeze for a moment, but I wish she'd do it again.

"Great show tonight," Sophia continues.

I'm still trying to process the fact that she initiated contact.

Progress.

She's coming around, or at least she wants to somewhere inside of her.

"Thanks," I pause. "Mind if I ask you a question?"

Sophia lifts her shoulder. "Sure," she says, taking a step back as if she's already afraid of my next words.

"Why did you come tonight?"

"Because I was invited," Sophia answered quickly.

She takes another step back, then a few more until her thighs bump against the sofa behind her. She grasps the sofa with her right hand, never once taking her eyes off of me.

I step tentatively toward Sophia, holding her gaze. I stop directly in front of her. Unfamiliar energy flows between us that I've never felt before. It's not only inviting. It's pure, raw, and calming. It boosts my courage.

"Did you come to see the band? Or did you come to see me?"

"The band," Sophia replied, glancing away and back at me.

I lift an eyebrow, feeling challenged. The look in Sophia's eyes tells a different story whether she wants to admit it or not.

"Being here with you is a nice bonus, though," Sophia continues. "I didn't think you'd...." Her voice trails off, and she blinks abnormally.

"That I'd what?"

"I thought that you would be occupied all night. That you wouldn't have time for me," Sophia pauses and offers a smile. "There's a lot of entertainment out there." She motions to the exit.

"Yet, I'm here with you." I lift her left hand to my lips and place a kiss on the back of it.

Sophia sucks in a breath, tightening her grip on the sofa. Her eyes fall to my hand, watching until I pull my lips away. I rub my thumb along the soft skin of her knuckles before releasing her hand.

I shouldn't have done that because now I want to do it again. I cross my arms over my chest to keep from doing just that.

Sophia stares at me with wonder and apprehension, and I can't look away. I wish I knew what she's not saying. It would make it a lot easier to move forward.

"When is bedtime?" I ask Sophia.

Her eyes widened. "Huh? What?"

"Bedtime?" I repeat, glancing at the door. "I'd like to call you to wish you a goodnight. If I don't get back out there soon, they might come searching," I explain.

"Right. Yeah. Bedtime." Sophia says, flustered. "I don't have one tonight. Ellis is sleeping over at Dalton's."

"So, you're alone. All night," I say, more for myself than her. I swallow the lump in my throat and shake the unkempt thoughts from my head.

"You could come over after the show if you're not too tired," Sophia offers.

"Are you sure?" I gently tip her chin up with my finger, staring deep into her eyes. "Because that will be the beginning of everything. There will be no going back."

I hold her gaze, hoping she understands exactly what that simple action would mean, not only for us but to everyone else. She has a child to consider, and if she's not ready to dive deeper into the limelight, it's probably not a good idea.

"I can't show up at your home without a meaning behind it, Soph. It's hard to keep a secret when the whole world is watching."

"I know, and I'm sure. I could use the company unless you've got somewhere better to be," Sophia challenges.

"And you think Dalton will be okay with this?"

Sophia shrugs, swallowing deeply. "We'll deal with him when the time comes," she says, throwing my words back at me.

I lean closer so that our lips are mere inches apart. Sophia doesn't pull away. Her gaze is intense, and I can tell that she wants whatever this is, but something is holding her back. Something is lurking in the back of her mind. I wonder what she'd do if a kiss were to grace her lips. Would she kiss me back or retaliate?

I clip her chin between my fingers, and her breath quickens. "In that case, send me your address," I say. "Let me know when you're home." I drop my hand and step back, needing to put space between us. "Or if you change your mind." I glance at her lips once more, then turn for the door.

Four

Sophia

I was the initiate.

I asked Owen to come over.

So why am I nervous? Why do I want to text him again and tell him not to come?

As bold moves go, this tops my chart. I never imagined Owen and me to be more than friends of friends. I've seen him a few times, but we had only met once before the pool party last week. So, yeah. He is blowing my mind. He seems like a decent guy, but then again, so did the last guy I dated.

I'm not sure what Owen's intentions are, and to be honest, I hadn't given it much thought because I don't know how serious I want us to be. I have a child to consider and a career that I love. I didn't come this far to have it all washed away. Whether Owen and I last past tonight or not, I intend to come out on the other side with everything still intact.

I rarely have time alone without my son, Ellis. He's at Dalton's during the day and back in my care moments after I'm off work. I've always been afraid of loosening the reins.

Tonight is about stepping out of my comfort zone, and I plan to enjoy it.

I turn the warm water on, streaming it into the bathroom sink. I bend down, cupping my hands under the water and splashing my face. I grab the towel from the holder on the wall, blotting away the damp spots. The towel comes down slowly as I stand upright and look in the mirror.

My hair still looks okay, but my face looks flushed. I haven't been able to think of anyone but Owen since he walked away from me at the club, and it shows. I tried showering and slipping into my comfy cotton shorts, but it didn't help.

My body stills at the sound of the doorbell ringing through the house.

Owen is here. Or at least it should be him. No one else would be at my door at this time of night or morning unless it were important. And he's the only other person I've given the security code recently.

I replace the towel and run my hands over my head, smoothing down the loose strands. A small, silent pep talk ensues as I give myself one last glance in the mirror.

The doorbell rings again as I approach, and I peep through the small window beside the door to be sure that it's Owen before opening it.

Owen stands before me, looking every bit as dapper as he did at the club. His fingers are stuffed into the pockets of his black jeans, lifting his shirt at the tail. He stares at me as if he's trying to figure me out.

Well, good luck with that.

I smile at the thought. I haven't even figured myself out yet, not entirely.

"Owen," I managed to say. "Come in." I step aside for him to enter.

"Hope I'm not too early or too late." Owen smiles back at me. A whiff of his cologne skims my nose as he enters. It reminds me of leather and summer rain. No traces of the sweat that I smelled earlier remain. He must've freshened up before coming over.

"You're right on time," I responded.

It's not like I had anything planned. I want all of my cards to be out of place tonight. I don't want to know what's coming next. I just want it to happen naturally. I'm open to just about anything.

"Can I get you a drink or a snack?" I asked.

"Water will be fine. I want to be sober for this," Owen says. He pulls his fingers from his pockets, rubbing the back of his neck. His confidence washes over me, giving me a small boost of my own.

I stare into Owen's watchful eyes, and I get it. I find every rumor about his eyes to be true. They're dark, intense, and while others might be inclined to look away, I refuse. I want to figure him out just as he does me.

"Coming right up. The living room is in there," I say, pointing to the opening behind Owen. "Make yourself comfortable."

I turn in the opposite direction toward the kitchen, and I feel the heat of his gaze as I walk. Once there, I grab two bottles of water, a bottle of red wine, and two glasses in case Owen changes his mind. Or if I need a little more courage. I'm usually more of a casual drinker, but tonight is different from all other times. There's a man in my home and not just any man. Owen is a commodity, highly sought after but never caught. And he wants me.

I hadn't let it sink in until now because he was always just a man—my brother's best friend. Someone I was attracted to but never dared to act on those feelings for more reasons than the obvious.

Owen is sitting in the center of the couch when I enter. His arms are outstretched over the back, and his legs widen to match.

I stop for a moment, swallowing deeply at the sight of him, and nearly dropping the glasses from my fingers in the process.

I gather my thoughts, completing my steps to the couch, and Owen takes the glasses and the bottle of wine from my grasp, setting them onto the coffee table. I place the water bottles next to them.

I'm not sure if I should sit next to Owen or across the room. He looks so inviting, but I don't want to be presumptuous. I glance at the spot to Owen's left, and he follows my gaze. One side of his lips tilts into a half-smile. Then those dark eyes return to mine.

"It's a risk, Soph." He shrugs.

I'm melting inside. I didn't bother to correct my name because it sounded so good falling from his mouth. I noticed at the club, and I definitely notice now how a single syllable resonates so much more than three. I ignore his warning and sit beside him, leaving a few inches between us.

What's next?

I stare at Owen, who's still watching me as if he can read my mind. It's the first time I've had a man over that wasn't my brother. It's the first time I've been close to a man since Ellis' father and I split up over five years ago. I now realize that five years is a long damn time.

"I'm all about taking risks tonight," I say, a bit more confident than I feel.

Owen replaces his arm on the couch behind me. He's not touching me anywhere, but it feels like he's touching me everywhere.

How is that possible?

"Why am I here, Soph?" Owen asks.

I blink rapidly, pulled from my trance. Owen's question caught me off guard, but I recovered quickly.

"You tell me. You pursued me, remember? I just provided a suitable meeting place."

Owen's eyebrows lift and fall. The smile vanishes from his face. He raises his right arm, and I freeze, my instinct telling me that I should be afraid, but I ignore it. The back of his fingers gently brushes the side of my cheek. My eyes fall shut, opening again when his hand moves away.

"What are you afraid of?" Owen asks.

"I'm not."

"Then why are you so tense?"

"I'm not afraid, Owen." I am tense with anticipation, though. I'm not used to being touched in a non-motherly way.

"So, whatever I suggest, you'll be cool with it?" Owen scoots closer, touching our legs together.

"You can suggest whatever you'd like. Guess we'll have to wait and see if I'm willing to take the risk." I shrug my shoulders innocently.

Owen glances at my mouth and back up to my eyes. He licks his lips, and a slight tremor moves through me. I kind of wish he'd kiss me and get it over with, but instead, he leans back a few inches.

"Tell me something about yourself," Owen says off-topic, throwing me for a loop.

"You want to know about me?"

"Yeah. You said anything I wanted. I want to get to know you."

"I'm not that interesting, Owen."

"Let me be the judge of that." Owen tugs gently at the braid trailing the center of my back, then lets it go.

"What do you want to know?" My body shifts to face him, bending one leg on the couch between us.

"If we're compatible," Owen says straight-faced. He glances at the wine bottle on the table and back at me. "I know that you like red wine. You have a son whom you're protective of. And you're not afraid to take chances because there's a practical stranger in your house at one in the morning." He pauses. "Tell me what makes you tick. What makes you happy? What makes you sad? I want to know everything."

"How much time do you have?" I responded playfully. A silly laugh spills from me, but Owen remains stoic.

"I've got all night. And the night after that. And the night after that. However long it takes. I'm here for it, Soph," Owen says seriously.

I stop laughing and clear my throat. All of my life, I've felt like an outsider. My Mom was the only one who ever seemed to care until Dalton came along. What I shared with Ellis' father wasn't real. He only cared about himself. He would've ruined me if I had stuck around.

But this feels different. Owen feels different. He came riding in like a knight in shining armor, and he wanted to know about me. I blow out a deep breath and rest my shoulder on the couch, wondering if I should let him in. I'm not a fan of being hurt again.

"I can do happy. You'll have to stick around a bit longer for the sad stuff," I tell Owen.

"I'll take whatever you're willing to give," he says, sincerely.

"Where do I begin?"

I look at the photo of Ellis and me on the wall behind Owen, and it brings a smile to my face. Ellis had just turned one when my mom took the picture. He was sitting on my lap, facing me with a huge grin on his face. My hands were at his sides, and Ellis pressed his tiny fingers against the sides of my face as I smiled back at him.

"Being a mom makes me happy," I say, focusing my eyes back on Owen. Ellis is the most important person in my life. So, Owen must understand that. He's a musician with no ties, a career that takes him away for weeks at a time, and I have a ready-made family. We are not ideal.

"Family makes me happy," I continue. "I like long walks and summer days. Movies that thrill me and books that make me cry." I close my eyes for a moment, thinking of everything that gives me joy. Owen stares at me with his head tilted to one side when I open them. There's a hint of a smile on his face. "What about you? What makes you happy?" I unconsciously tap Owen's thigh with my hand.

"My music," Owen says instantly. "It's been a part of my life for so long. I wouldn't know what to do without it. I think of it as family. I love it. Sometimes I need a break from it, but I could never abandon it," he says with a smile.

I like that he loves what he does for a living. His passion for music is clear in his eyes.

"Do you enjoy your job?" Owen asks.

"I do," I say without hesitation. "It's not what I thought I'd be doing when I was younger." A grin bubbled out of me, thinking of how different things could've been if I had gone to pilot school instead.

Owen's eyebrow rises. "And what was that?"

"Don't laugh, but I wanted to be a pilot. I wanted to travel the world."

"So why didn't you?"

"I gave it up for love. Or what I thought was love at the time." My mouth twists at the thought. "Ellis' father was a real charmer."

And an even bigger ass.

"Is he still around?"

"No." I shake my head. "I broke things off before Ellis was born."

Owen stares at me as if he wants to ask what happened, but he doesn't.

"Are you seeing anyone else?" He asks instead.

I shake my head no again. "After...." I pause, not wanting to disclose too much, and run Owen away. My problems are my own. "I didn't see the point. I had Ellis, and he was all that mattered."

"And now? Do you see a point in letting me in?" Owen asks.

"Well, you've gotten further than anyone else. I'd say that's more than a point."

"Why me? Why now?" Owen's thumb moves over the back of the couch. His hands are so close to my shoulder, but so far.

"Now, because you asked nicely." I smile. "You, because you seem like an okay guy. My brother trusts you, and as far as I've heard, you've never steered him wrong."

I grab a water bottle from the table and take a few sips.

Conversation with Owen comes easily like we've been doing it for years instead of minutes. I don't need the wine as I suspected I would.

"So, what do you do for fun?" Owen tilts his head to the right, studying me. His eyes focus on mine every chance that I allow it.

"Absolutely nothing." To be honest, being here with Owen is the most grown-up fun I've had in a very long time. "My life is a routine. I find it easier that way."

Owen eyes me curiously. "Is there something that you want to do?"

"Sure, but…."

"You like easy, uncomplicated," Owen finishes my sentence, and I wonder if he is, in fact, a mind reader.

"Are you an only child?" I ask, changing the subject.

"Enough about you, huh?" Owen chuckles. "To answer your question, yes. It's just me, my mom, and dad." His smile wanes as he picks up the water bottle from the table and opens it, taking a huge gulp. He sets the bottle back down, and I set my bottle beside his. He settles back onto the couch, placing his hands onto his thighs.

I can't stand the tension any longer. Our questions seem to be getting more personal by the minute, and I don't see the point in complicating things if this is a one-night stand. I know what Owen said, but guys say things all the time to get what they want. We're both adults capable of making mature decisions.

"What do you want, Owen?" I ask seriously. "What are we doing here? Is this a fling, or do you want to try because I'm okay with either? I just have to know for sure."

Owen's eyes burn into mine, and I shudder inside at the weight of his stare.

"What do I want?" Owen questions. "I want to see what we can become," he says, motioning between us. "What we have, what we're doing is not a fling unless you want it to be."

Owen takes my left hand in his left, scooting closer to me. He slides his thumb over my ring finger, stopping at my knuckle. I can't tell if it means more than just an action or not, but the action causes my breath to pause. He raises his right hand and tilts my chin up with his fingers. I try to control my breathing, but I'm not sure if it's working or not.

"What I want," Owen says, a hair away from my lips.

I want you to kiss me.

"I want to fall asleep with you enclosed in my arms and wake up with no regrets," Owen continues. "I want to kiss you without feeling like I don't deserve it."

Whether Owen deserves a kiss or not is the furthest thing from my mind. I deserve it. I want it, and that should be enough. I didn't realize how much I've missed a man's touch.

"Kiss me," I say breathlessly, staring into Owen's eyes.

Owen's fingers are still tilting my chin, and I'm enjoying the feel of his warm skin against mine. His thumb moves between our lips, brushing over mine. Wariness shows on his face, and I wonder why.

I've given Owen the green light, and he still hesitates, but I can tell that he wants to taste my lips just as bad as I want him to.

Maybe he's having second thoughts. So, I asked him, "What are you afraid of?"

Owen swallows, his thumb moving over my lips again as he gives my hand that he's holding a subtle squeeze.

"Is that what you think, Soph? That I'm afraid?"

"Yes," I lied, trying to get a rise out of him. I know that he's not scared, but there has to be something holding him back.

"You have no idea. No idea," Owen responds, moving his hand to my cheek. He lets go of my other hand, bringing his hand up to my other cheek. His eyes seem to turn fiery, and my body feels like molten lava.

I sense the shift in slow motion as Owen moves closer to me. I suck in a shallow breath and blow it out. Owen catches it as his lips meet mine. My eyes fall shut at the soft press of his mouth on mine. His tongue teases my mouth open, and I moan softly.

I knew it was coming, but the shock isn't any less jarring. My fingers dig into Owen's thighs as my appetite for more grows stronger.

Owen's hands drop to my waist, nudging me closer. The closer I get, the more I struggle for air. I pull away from his lips, needing to catch my breath. My heart pounds inside my chest as I stare into his eyes. A flash of something old haunts my vision, but I push it away.

Owen is different.

"Will you stay?" I ask Owen.

"As long as you want me to," Owen replied.

Be bold. Be brave.

It's hard to do any of those things with Owen watching me the way he is, but I attempt anyway.

Owen's hands slide across my thighs as I stand. There's not one hint of a smile on his face. He's the most intense person I've ever encountered, and that scares me and excites me at the same time.

I hold my hand out for his, and he grabs hold, standing in front of me. I turn for the hallway and begin walking toward my bedroom. The silence between us has never been so loud. More unspoken questions are asked in the seven seconds it takes to enter my bedroom than we've asked all night.

I stop when we reach the bed and turn to Owen. I step out of my shorts, leaving my shirt on. A moment passes between us before I step around him and pull the comforter back on the bed. Then, I climb in, scooting to the left side, and wait.

I swallow back the uncertainty as Owen pulls his shirt over his head and again when he steps out of his pants, leaving only his boxers on.

Owen is solid muscle, chiseled in all of the right places. A six-pack of hard abs with a healthy-sized log beneath stares back at me. My eyes snap up to his, still intense, without a smile.

Owen gets into the bed, then leans in to kiss me. It's a simple, effective kiss that only lasts for seconds before he pulls away.

"Turn around," Owen instructs.

Without question, I do as he says, laying my head on his outstretched arm.

Owen drapes his other arm over my side, flattening his palm over my belly and pulling my back against his chest.

I suck in a breath, and it seems to get lodged there as I gather my thoughts. Blowing it out, I relax onto Owen, and he settles around me. His breath tickles the side of my neck from behind, and I wait, expecting so much more.

A few quiet minutes pass before I notice Owen's breathing even out, and a subtle snore sneaks in between. His snoring is kind of adorable, and it would've made me smile if I weren't so confused.

I glance over my shoulder, and Owen's arms tighten around me. I settle back into position, closing my eyes and trying to calm my raging heartbeat and clear my mind.

Five

Owen

Sophia is still in my arms when I wake up the next morning, but I can feel that she's awake.

I had to force myself to sleep last night to refrain from doing what I wanted to do. I didn't expect her to take her shorts off after how she had reacted the few times that we'd met. She put on a hell of a show last night, but I didn't trust it one bit.

I snuggle as close to Sophia as I can get, breathing into the side of her neck through my nose. I kiss the back of her neck. "No regrets," I say close to her ear. "Good morning."

Sophia's cheekbone rises as she says, "Good morning. I would turn around, but I don't want to knock you out with my breath."

"I'm sure it's not that bad," I say, chuckling.

"I'd rather not risk it," Sophia pauses. "May I ask you a question?"

"Anything," I responded.

"Last night I thought that you, that we.... When you woke up, you said, *'no regrets.'* Does that mean sleeping with me would've been regretful?"

Sophia quiets, and I can feel her body tense under my touch. The last thing that I wanted was to make her feel unwanted because that's the opposite of what I feel.

"Quite the contrary," I tell Sophia. "Sleeping with you was the highlight of my night. Having sex with you would've been a regret."

Sophia tries to move out of my arms, but I pull her back.

"Not for the reasons you think, though."

"And how do you know what I'm thinking?" Sophia asks with a hint of sass and frustration.

"Wise man, remember?" I loosen my grip on her, giving her the freedom to move about. "Turn around, Soph."

A few seconds pass before Sophia turns to face me. She covers her mouth with her right hand, and I pull it away. I push her hair behind her ear with my fingers. Then, I rest my hand on her hip.

"You're so damn cute," I tell her, bringing a small blush to her cheeks.

"Just cute?" Sophia questions.

"You're beautiful too, but the ugliest person can be beautiful on the outside. It takes someone special to pull off cute."

"I guess that makes you adorable then," Sophia teases.

I've never met anyone quite like her before. One minute she's pulling away from me, and the next, she's offering to share her bed. I'm intrigued.

"Can I speak candidly?" I ask, and she nods. "I want to fuck you."

Sophia swallows deeply to my confession, and her hand twitches at my side.

"I would like nothing more than to take advantage of every inch of your body, and physically I can tell that you want that too. But mentally, you're not ready."

Sophia looks away as if she knows exactly what I'm talking about. I wish I could see inside her mind to know what she's thinking.

I guide her gaze back to me. "That's why I would regret it," I continue. "I want you to be comfortable. Drop all of the armor. You have to be who you are with me if this will work, Soph. You have to learn to trust me with whatever. I promise I can handle it." I brush my thumb softly over her cheek. "Think you can do that?"

Sophia smiles, though it doesn't quite reach her eyes. "I can try."

"Good because I could get used to this," I say, pulling her closer. I wrap my arms around her, kissing her forehead, lingering there for a few seconds before pulling away. I need to get out of her bed, but I'm not ready to leave her.

"Speaking of," Sophia says. "Would you like to stay awhile? I could call Dalton and maybe pick Ellis up later."

"I'd like that, but only if Ellis doesn't mind being away from you longer." I don't want to be the guy who takes the kid away from his mom. I want to be a welcomed addition.

"Are you kidding? Ellis has been begging me for sleepovers and more time with friends. I'm the one with attachment issues." Sophia's eyes pop open, and she covers her face with one hand. "I probably shouldn't have said that. I promise I won't turn into a stalker." She giggles.

Covering her face seems to be a coping mechanism for Sophia when she's embarrassed. I grab her hand from her face, entwining our fingers together and moving them down to our sides, but not letting go.

"I wouldn't mind you being attached to me," I say, wiggling my eyebrows, which makes her blush even more.

Sophia tries to lift her hand but relaxes when I rub my thumb over hers.

"It's okay, Soph. I want to see every blush that stains your cheeks, especially if I put it there."

Sophia giggles like a schoolgirl. "I should probably brush my teeth now and make that call."

"Does my breath offend you?" I chuckle.

"Don't be silly. We're like a seasoned married couple now," Sophia teases, making me speechless for the first time since we've met.

I've thought about settling down before, and I've imagined Sophia being the woman standing in front of me at the altar. The fact that she's joking about it means that she's thought about it too. We're nowhere near ready for that, but the thought is still mind-opening.

Sophia's eyes widened. "I'm going to go now."

I let go of her hand as she moved to get out of bed. She brings me a new toothbrush after a few minutes. Then she calls Dalton to ask if Ellis can stay a while.

· · · · · ♩ ♪ · · · · ·

Sophia and I spent the morning and afternoon in a mix of talking, kissing, and stolen touches until the tension became too much. Now she's lying on her bed, and I'm on the floor leaning against the bed, trying to remind myself why I didn't have sex with her. *Because she's not ready.* My eyes focus on the green and blue curtains hanging in front of the window as I try to calm my hormones.

Regardless of how I'm feeling right now, I don't regret my decision, and I'm still not ready to leave her. But the receding sun won't let me forget that it's nearing that time.

"Soph," I say, turning my head to look at her on the bed.

"Owen," she says, a gracious smile curving her lips.

She's probably thinking about our last make-out session that landed me on the floor. I need to think of something less sexy and quick.

"Can I ask you a more personal question?"

Sophia sits up, bracing her body on her elbows. "Throw it at me," she says, tweaking an eyebrow.

I hesitate for a moment, unsure if now is the right time. Sophia's father is dead, and though he provided for her financially, he was never there physically. Being the man he was, I doubt she would have wanted to know him, but I'm curious.

"Did you hate your father for not being around?"

The smile drops from Sophia's face, and she sits up fully, swinging her legs over the edge of the bed. She looks down at me, clearing her throat. Then her eyes turn to the same window I'd been staring at before. Her brows knit together as if she's trying to come up with the right words, and when they pull apart, her eyes return to mine.

"My father," Sophia says, pausing. "Before my preteen years, I spent more time hating my mother than him because I thought that she was keeping him away from me. When I was old enough to understand, my mother sat me down and told me their whole sordid story." Her lips curve down. "I still blamed her for sleeping with a married man, but my anger eventually subsided, and all I felt was sadness. Knowing the truth made me feel dirty because I was the product of a lie. A lie that we could never let get out. As for my father, I didn't feel the need to waste energy hating someone I never knew. He was just a donor and a bad one at that. Knowing what I know now, I count myself lucky that he wasn't a part of my everyday life."

Sophia sighs heavily, and I blow out a breath with her.

"I'm sorry, Soph."

"Don't be. I had a great life," Sophia offers a sad smile. "There is a bright side to all of it," she adds, placing her hand on my shoulder. "If they hadn't cheated, I wouldn't be here, Dalton wouldn't be my brother, I wouldn't have the best stepmom in the world, and I never would've known you. I've gained so much more as a result of his death than I ever did when he was alive. The dirt is still thick, but it's a little cleaner now."

"I like the bright side," I tell Sophia. I take her hand in mine, pulling her down to me. Then I kiss her like my life depends on it.

Six

Sophia

I'm still young, but I feel it for the first time in a long time. Owen kissed me as if he would never see me again before we parted. An hour later, my lips are still on fire, and my heart hasn't found a steady beat.

I park my car in front of Dalton's garage and look into the rearview mirror, trying to force the giddiness away. Even in the darkness, it still shines bright. I don't know if I can hide it. I don't know if I want to. But I know why I'm considering it.

I'm afraid of my past and what could happen if it catches up to me.

I clear my throat, and my smile diminishes.

Works every time.

Just when I allow myself a reprieve, Ellis' father, Kenneth, is always there in the back of my mind to remind me how easily my world can be shattered. I left him, but he never left me.

I unconsciously touch my neck, dropping my hand on a sigh. I get out of my car and walk to the front door, ringing the bell.

Dalton answers, swinging the door wide for me to enter. He closes the door behind me and steps to my side as I turn to face him.

"Thanks for letting Ellis sleep over," I tell Dalton.

"No need to thank me. Ellis is my nephew. He's welcome anytime," Dalton replies.

Dalton has made it clear that Ellis and I are both welcomed to his home, and though we've grown closer over the past two years, I still have outsider syndrome sometimes—like I don't belong in his world.

"By the way, where is he?" I ask, looking around. The house is quiet, with no signs that children are inside.

"Upstairs with Josie in the playroom." Dalton looks toward the stairs, then at me. He crosses his arms over his chest, eyeing me closely. "Everything okay?" he asks.

"Sure, why wouldn't it be?" I say defensively. "Did you hear something?"

Dalton shrugs, rubbing his chin between his fingers. "You seem different, is all. And you let the kid out of your sight for the night," he jokes.

Am I that transparent?

I shuffle my feet nervously. Just the thought of Dalton finding out about Owen and me has me anxious. It shouldn't matter what he thinks. I'm a grown woman. I can handle myself. But a part of me wants his approval.

"I'm great. Something urgent came up. A new...." I pause, searching for the proper word.

Project.

No. The word feels too mechanical, like a must-do.

Boyfriend.

Hmm. Maybe. However, Owen is certainly not a boy.

I just realized that Owen and I never labeled our relationship. We agreed that we liked each other. We agreed that we wanted to try, but what does that mean? I furrow my forehead.

What the hell are we?

"Sophia," Dalton called.

"Yeah," I answered, snapping out of it. "A new assignment came up," I continued. It's not a lie at all. This thing between Owen and me needs figuring out. I want to study him. "I may need your sitter's contact info. My assignment may be an ongoing thing," I finish.

"Whatever you need. I'm here," Dalton proclaims without question.

"Hey, you two," Joselyn beamed, coming down the stairs with Brodie on her hip and Ellis following behind. "I thought I heard your voice," she said, looking directly at me.

"Hey." I shift my body toward them. Then I held my arms open for Ellis when his feet hit the floor. He runs to me, throwing his arms around my waist.

"Mom!" Ellis exclaims.

"I missed you too, Bud," I confess, ruffling his hair.

Joselyn passes Brodie off to Dalton, giving him a peck on his lips in the process. "Will you take the boys for a few minutes and give us girls time to talk?" She asked him.

"On one condition," Dalton bargained. "Don't corrupt my sister," he chuckles.

"Hey," Joselyn feigns offense.

I smile, loving the way they are together.

Our father was in Dalton's life, but their relationship wasn't a good one. So, I'm glad that he found happiness despite our messed-up world.

I give Ellis a gentle squeeze, then release him. "Go with Dalton," I instructed, kissing the top of his head.

As soon as they're out of sight, Joselyn grabs my wrist and pulls me in the opposite direction. She pulls a stool out from the bar, drops my wrist, and nods to the stool.

"Have a seat," Joselyn says, stepping around the bar.

I squint my eyes at her and her suspicious behavior.

Joselyn, her best friend Rose, and her sister Katie accepted me into their lives from the moment we met, and we've all grown quite close. I've learned that it's hard to keep anything from Joselyn during that time. She picks up on the most minute details. I guess that's why she's so good at her job.

My eyes widen as she faces me with narrowed eyes. Dalton doesn't read the tabloids, but it's Joselyn's job to be on top of the latest news. I wonder if she knows. I live outside the city, where my nearest neighbor is a quarter-mile away. Large trees and tall fences outline my property. Even when the news about Dalton and I got out, the media eventually died down. They've followed Dalton to my home, but never me alone. I suppose someone could've been lurking when Owen came knocking after the show.

My eyes return to normal, and I square my shoulders. "What's up?"

"Where to start?" Joselyn taunts. "Ellis stayed over. Relaxed posture. How about the smile that you're trying desperately to hide? And let's not forget the glow," she speculates. "Who's the guy? Was it someone from the club?" She asks.

So, she doesn't know. Not yet.

I look over my shoulder at the opening to ensure that we're alone. Then I look back at Joselyn, placing my palms flat on the countertop. There's no use in trying to hide it from her.

"So, it was a guy from the club," I began, smiling.

"Is he nice? Is he cute? Is he?" Joselyn pauses, wiggling her eyebrows.

"Rose is rubbing off on you," I claim. A laugh topples out of me, and I bring my hand to my mouth to quiet it. Dropping my hand, I say dreamily, "He's all of those things."

"How did you pull that off? You were with us the whole night except for that one trip to the bathroom." Joselyn surveys me. Then her mouth opens wide. "Did you? Did you screw some stranger in a public bathroom?" She asks.

I gasp. "No. No, it was nothing like that. More like a friendly run-in in the dressing room," I defend, biting my bottom lip.

"Dressing room," Joselyn says. "Wait." Her eyes flashed with understanding, and her jaw dropped open as her hands slapped the counter. "Owen!" She whisper-shouts.

"Shh." I look over my shoulder and back again. "Dalton doesn't know."

"Well, duh." Joselyn exaggerates. "You know I can't keep this from him, right? We don't keep secrets, Sophia," She warns.

"I know, but it's still so new. I don't want to rock the boat unless it's necessary. Can you hold off for a few days, until we're sure?" I ask.

Joselyn pursed her lips, her eyes glancing behind me. "A few days. A week tops, if you have that long. You're probably already in today's news," She sighs. "I'll try to keep him away from his mother. Ruth uses the news as a morning wake-up call," she chuckles.

I reach over the counter, covering Joselyn's hands with mine. "Thanks."

"No need to thank me. You and Owen," Joselyn said unbelievingly. "One of you needs to tell Dalton before the world does."

"We will," I promise, pulling my hand back.

Joselyn's mouth curves into a smile. "I'm glad it's you," she says.

"What do you mean?" I ask, tilting my head to the side.

"With Owen. He's a good guy. You're a great woman. The two of you together…." Joselyn's words trail off as she mimics the sound of an explosion with her hands, demonstrating the action. "I see a triple date in our future," she predicts.

I laugh because it's funny and kind of unreal that we're even talking about this.

Owen and me.

Not even I would've guessed.

Seven

Owen

The last four days have been a learning curve, a true test of my patience and resistance. Hearing Sophia's sweet voice every night and not being able to see or touch her is driving me insane. My emotions are all over the place—wanting her near me and the need to shelter her and Ellis at the same time. Luckily, nothing has leaked in the news yet, but Sophia told me that Joselyn knows. So, it's only a matter of time before everyone else does too.

My cell phone pings, and I let my guitar strap rest around my neck to check the message. The name on the screen brings a smile to my face.

Melody.

It's the incognito name that I gave Sophia on my phone to protect us from prying eyes.

Melody: We could have a reveal party ;)

I chuckle under my breath at her suggestion.

Last night we played with silly ideas about publicizing our relationship on the phone. Her idea is by far is the best bad idea yet.

Me: Like the premise, but I'll pass. Are you still coming over?

Sophia is bringing Ellis over to Dalton's house to play with Brodie and Jasper for a little while. The guys and I are about to begin a practice session.

Melody: Yes

We had also juggled with ways to sneak around while she was here. I stare at her response, my heart pounding in my chest.

Me: Can't wait to see you.

Luke snatches the cell phone from my hand and starts reading the message on the screen. "Who is Melody?" he asks.

I jump to my feet, taking the phone back before he sees too much. Then, I lock the screen.

"Melody?" Dalton questions as he enters the studio.

I don't say a word. I glare at Luke for interrupting my good mood, and he laughs. Luke has always been a jokester and a pain in everyone's ass. Getting married only dampened him a little.

"Whoever she is, Owen can't wait to see her," Luke says humorously. I'm contemplating driving my fist into his arm.

"Where did you meet this, Melody?" Dalton asks, catching my attention.

I swallow hard, deciding to go with the truth. "At Lonzo's," I say, eyeing them both.

"So, you made it personal," Luke concludes. "My man. It's about time. I was starting to feel sorry for the lone ranger in the group," he teases.

Dalton laughs. "If you need any help with Melody, let me know."

In this instance, it's not funny. I freeze for a moment, thinking back to when I teased Dalton that same offer when he and Joselyn started dating. If he knew who Melody truly was, he'd be sick that he'd even played around with the idea.

"I don't need your help," I tell Dalton. Luke opens his mouth to speak, and I cut him off. "You either, Luke. Besides, Rose would kill you before that happens," I say pointedly.

Luke snaps his mouth shut, gaining a laugh from Dalton and me.

"Fuck you," Luke says, chuckling after a few seconds.

"Alright. Alright. Let's get started," Dalton demands.

Luke and I fall in line, and we begin to play. I'm not as distracted as I was before Sophia and I made things official. Knowing that there's a real chance for us makes the music flow smoother. Practice lasts just past an hour, and I'm excited when it's over because I know that Sophia is at the main house. I'm hoping to test out one of those bad ideas tonight.

Dalton and Luke enter the house before me, walking over to their wives and giving them a not-so-subtle kiss. My eyes find Sophia sitting in the singles recliner alone. Her back is to me, so I can't see her expression, but I imagine it matched mine before I looked away from the married folks. Disgusted. Uncomfortable.

I walk up behind Sophia and discreetly trail my finger along the base of her neck. Her body stiffens, but she doesn't turn around. I hear a small intake of breath from her that makes me smile. The back of my hand brushes her arm as I step to the side of the chair.

Bad idea number one.

I sit on the arm of Sophia's chair and glance down at her. The kissing has stopped across the room, but the affection hasn't. I'm usually able to block them out, but that's hard to do with Sophia so close. It's a reminder of everything I want to do with her but can't at the moment.

Sophia clears her throat. "Owen, I don't feel welcome in this room. We should probably go check on the kids," she says loud enough for everyone to hear.

That gets Dalton's attention. He looks our way, his eyes focused on Sophia. "I'll go," he says, glancing at me.

I don't miss the warning look Joselyn shoots Sophia or the caution in Dalton's stare. It's his protective look—the one that says stay away. He gave me the same look when I asked if he needed help with Joselyn.

Telling Dalton about us will be interesting, but he's going to have to learn to accept it because I'm not giving Sophia up, not when we've just begun. I can't give her up.

"Yeah, go. Check on the kids," Joselyn says to Dalton. She pats his thigh to get his attention. He smiles when he looks at her, then gets up and leaves the room, giving me a final glance.

The room is quiet for a few moments after Dalton leaves.

"Was I the only one who saw that?" Luke questions, breaking through the silence.

"Saw what," Joselyn asks.

"The evil eye that Dalton gave Owen," Luke answers, looking my way. "You should probably stick with Melody and leave that one alone," Luke says to me while nodding to Sophia.

Sophia stiffens next to me. Then her eyes find mine. A small frown of disappointment appears on her face before she turns away.

I need to explain. I can't have Sophia thinking that there's someone else. What Dalton thinks is the least of my worries right now.

Before I have the chance, Sophia stands and walks out of the living room.

Rose gasps, sitting forward on the couch. "Oh my God," she says, looking at me. "She likes you," she says, pointing at the empty opening that Sophia just walked through.

I rise from the arm of the chair and leave the room without a response, rounding the corner just in time to see the glass door slide closed. I follow Sophia outside, closing the door behind me. The moon is out, but the sun has yet to make its exit.

Sophia is standing to my right, a few feet from the door, with her back facing the house. One hand is in her jeans pocket, while the other hangs at her side. Her head turns in my direction. Then she looks away. I walk toward her, intent on trying to get her to understand. I stop, facing her with my hands at my side.

"Soph, please let me explain."

Sophia shakes her head. "You don't have to."

It's twisted, but I love the hurt on her face just as much as I hate it. She's jealous. I'm intrigued.

"I need to. I should have told you about Melody." I smirk, and Sophia glares at me.

"What game are you playing, Owen? I thought...." Sophia pauses, looking away from me and crossing her arms over her belly.

I place my finger under her chin, guiding her eyes back to mine. "You *are* my Melody, Soph. If there's a game to be played, it's with you."

Sophia looks confused, her eyes narrowing on me. I lean in closer, and her back presses against the side of the house.

"I saved you as Melody on my phone. Luke saw your message earlier."

Understanding dawns in Sophia's eyes. "Owen," she whispers.

I tilt my head and kiss her before she can say another word. I kiss her because I can't hold back any longer. I kiss her because it feels right and wrong and forbidden. My arms wrap around her waist, pulling her close, and she leans into me.

Sophia's hands are trapped between us, and palms flattened against my chest.

I pull away after a few seconds, breathing labored, heart trembling. My fingers trail smoothly up and down Sophia's back.

Bad idea number two.

"Four days," I say, gazing into her eyes. "Let's not do that again, Melody."

"Let's not," Sophia agrees breathlessly.

I step back when I hear the door slide open. Joselyn peeks her head out, staring at us.

Sophia straightens, looking back at her. "I know," she says. "Can you give us a minute?" She asks Joselyn.

"It doesn't take long to check on the kids," Joselyn says, clearly annoyed. She disappears inside, and the door closes.

I get it. Joselyn doesn't feel comfortable keeping secrets after what happened with her and Dalton, and it isn't fair to expect her to. It's our mess. We need to clean it up.

"Are you ready for this?" I ask Sophia.

"Are you?" She counters.

I smirk. "So damn cute," I say, kissing Sophia's forehead. "Come on."

We walk to the back door together, and Sophia steps inside first. She returns to her place in the recliner, and I return to mine next to her. Every eye in the room is focused on us, but I don't care.

Dalton enters seconds later with a huge grin on his face. "The kids are fine. Jasper has everything under control." He sits next to Joselyn, and we remain quiet.

"Luke, let's go grab a drink. I'm thirsty," Rose says. They stand, and Luke looks like he wants to object, but he could never say no to Rose.

"I'm a bit parched myself," Joselyn says, standing with them. "Want anything," She asks Dalton.

"No," Dalton answers, squinting his eyes. He stares at us after they leave. "Why does it feel like I'm the only one that's not in on the secret?" He asks.

"Owen and I are dating," Sophia blurts out, stunning both of us. My gaze falls on her, and she grabs my hand.

I was hoping to ease Dalton into the idea, but apparently, Sophia had other plans. I relax, wrapping my hand in hers. There's no going back now, not after this.

"I wanted you to hear it from me," Sophia continues. "Before you say anything, it's my decision, and I understand the risks."

I give her hand a gentle squeeze letting her know that I'm with her.

"Okay," Dalton says, but I know him well. He is not fine with this. "Mind if I speak with Owen alone?" He asks Sophia.

"I do," Sophia responds, sighing. "But I know it's going to happen anyway, whether it's now or later, objection or not."

Sophia looks up at me and smiles when she stands. She places a sweet kiss on my lips, in front of her brother and my best friend. Then, she walks over to Dalton, and I hear her say, "Try not to ruin a good thing for me, will you?"

Dalton clears his throat without responding. The room quiets when Sophia is gone, and I'm unsure if I should speak first or wait for Dalton. He's always been like a brother to me. So, I would hate for this to come between us.

Dalton's hand grips the arm of the couch. "How long?" He grinds out.

I've seen Dalton angry before, so I choose my words carefully when I say, "It's not what you think. We're taking things slow."

Dalton grips the arm of the couch a little tighter, but I don't back down. That's not what we do. We talk things out. We come to an understanding, whether we fully agree or not. We are family.

Dalton tilts his head slightly. "How long have you been keeping this from me?" He asks, his expression morphing from anger to hurt.

"I ran into her after the show the other night, and we talked. I gave her my number, and we've been talking ever since." I leave out the part where I showed up at her job, the night we spent together, the touching and kissing.

"So, it was you—the assignment that popped up," He states.

Assignment?

Sophia called me her assignment. I stand and sit down in the recliner, staring across the room. It's kind of hot. For some reason, that makes me smile inside, but I remain stoic on the outside. The last thing that I need is for Dalton to think this is a joke to me.

"I wanted to tell you, Dalton, but I needed to be sure Sophia was ready," I say.

"Are you ready?" Dalton asks, seriously, his fingers relaxing on the arm of the chair. He shifts, throwing one arm over the back of the couch.

"I've been ready," I say without hesitation. "You know I've always wanted a family. And since I met Sophia, I've never been more willing to try and make it work with someone," I answer truthfully. "I can't explain it, but she's special." She's always been special. That's why I stayed away.

Dalton stares at me for a long moment, and I remain quiet, allowing him time to process his feelings. I know this isn't easy for him after what he's gone through with his father and finally connecting with his sister. It makes sense that he would want to protect her, but he doesn't have to protect her from me.

"And Ellis, how do you feel about him? Because it's not just you and Sophia, Owen. If you do this, it'll be you, Sophia, and Ellis," Dalton finally speaks. "This isn't something you can easily walk away from."

"I have no plans of walking away, and I adore Ellis, even though he gave me the evil eye," I chuckle.

Dalton raised an eyebrow, a proud, fleeting smile appearing on his face. "He's a great kid, and Sophia has been through enough. I only want to protect her," he sighs, rubbing a hand down his face. His eyes return to me, stern but understanding. "I know you, Owen. I know that you're not one to break hearts—not on purpose at least," he says with a smirk. Dalton leans forward, resting his elbows on his knees. "I need you to promise me that you won't hurt Sophia. Promise that she and Ellis will be safe with you."

I swallow hard at the raw emotion in his voice. I don't know everything that Sophia has been through, but I wonder if Dalton does, judging by the seriousness of his tone.

"It's my mission to be the man that they need. I promise that I'll be good to them if they'll have me," I say.

Dalton nods, leaning back onto the couch. "Just do me one favor," he says.

"What's that?"

"Don't kiss her in front of me," Dalton responds, and we both chuckle.

"I can't make any promises," I say, happy that we were able to talk this through. Glad that Sophia and I don't have to hide anymore, and I can fall for her in the limelight.

Eight

Sophia

I've always wanted to send flowers but never had anyone to send them to. You are my someone, my Melody. This is our moment.

I smiled giddily at Owen's words on the card that came with the roses he sent to my job for the umpteenth time today. Nothing has changed since we broke the news to Dalton yesterday, yet, everything has. Owen has never sent flowers, and I've never received any until now. I haven't gotten this much eye contact at work since they all found out that Dalton was my brother. I can only imagine the looks and whispers when they find out who the man behind the roses is.

I slip the card into my purse and pull the strap over my shoulder. I grab the crystal vase, positioning it in my left arm. The aroma from the petals lingers near my nostrils as I open my office door and close it behind me. A fist full of nerves settles in my gut as I walk through the main office and out the door.

I set the vase in the passenger seat and pulled the seat belt over it to keep it steady. A series of ups and downs, smiles and frowns, assault me on the way home. I like Owen, and I want us to work, but it doesn't stop the doubt. It doesn't keep me from asking myself, over and over, if I'm doing the right thing. Being with him will cause my demons to surface, and I'm unsure if I'm prepared to face them.

Before Ellis was born, I made promises that I would always be there to protect him, to love him no matter what, and never let anything cloud my judgment ever again. I promised that we'd live a simple life surrounded by people who loved us. Now I'm wondering if it's possible to keep those promises.

I kick my shoes off by the front door and walk into the kitchen, placing the vase on the countertop. The house is quiet, empty, unusually so.

I dropped Ellis off at Dalton's this morning because he asked to go for the weekend. Owen will be here soon, and even though Ellis wanted to leave, I still feel guilty, like I'm filling in the gaps with someone else while he's away. I wonder if that feeling will ever subside. It's been the two of us for so long. I wonder how Ellis will feel when he finds out about Owen.

I pour myself a small glass of wine and down it in one shot. I settle on the barstool, looking outside through the kitchen window. I'm nervous—a feeling that only seems to surface when Owen is involved. We've been official for about a week, and we've talked plenty, but we've barely seen each other. Will spending more time together bring out the worst in us?

A half-hour passes with me sitting there overthinking everything before the doorbell rings.

Owen's hands are stuffed into the back pockets of his jeans when I open the door. A charcoal tee hangs just below his hips. His lips curve into a smile as he looks me up and down. An oversized bag is draped over his left shoulder. I smile back at him, thinking of how right he is.

Owen is a risk, but isn't everything?

"I brought my own toothbrush," Owen says with a sly smirk.

My heart thumps, and my hand slips from the doorknob momentarily.

Who knew that something as simple as a toothbrush could bring me so much joy?

"Come in," I manage to say around the lump in my throat.

Owen steps inside, stopping near the door. An awkward feeling passes between us, and I can't decide what to do next for the life of me.

"Soph," Owen says, stepping closer to me. He brushes his thumb over my cheek, staring into my eyes. A tremor moves through my body as I stare back at him. "Stop overthinking," Owen continues. "I don't expect anything. If your presence is all you have to give right now, then that's all I need."

I swallow hard, blinking away my mind freeze.

"Thank you for the roses. They were the talk of the office today," I say, trying to get my mind off his hands that are still on me.

"Happy to appease." Owen pulls his hand away, tapping the bag at his side. "Guest or master?" he asks.

"Master," I say too quickly. "Unless you'd prefer...."

"Master it is," Owen winks.

He winks, and I stumble back over my feet. I close my eyes, bracing for impact. For a moment, I think that my cheeks will hit the floor, but Owen catches me. Our bodies crash together, and a gush of breath leaves me. I open my eyes slowly, my body bent backward in Owen's arms, and my feet half off the floor.

"I've got you," Owen says.

At that moment, I felt a weight lift. I felt as if I had waited my entire life to hear those words—to have someone say them and mean it.

"I'll always catch you, Soph." Owen guides my body up so that I'm standing straight again, but he doesn't let go, and I don't want him to.

I tip up on my toes to kiss him, bringing my hands to his cheeks. Owen kisses me back, linking his tongue with mine and pulling me closer. He makes me forget everything. Makes me want more.

My chest rises and falls quickly when Owen pulls away. An objection is on the tip of my tongue, but I clamp my mouth shut—and my legs too.

"Red wine," Owen says, licking his lips.

I'm confused for a moment. Then, I remembered the pre-party. I shrug. "I kind of started without you," I told Owen.

"We need to work on getting me caught up then," Owen teases, sliding his palm down my arm and joining my hand with his.

I pull him toward my bedroom, and he sets his bag on the floor by the bed once we're inside.

Owen looks at me with dreamy eyes that say so much without saying anything at all. "Let's pretend," he says, causing me to raise an eyebrow. Owen turns us so that I'm facing the bed. Then, he sits at the foot, pressing his palms into the covers. "Let's pretend," he says again, "that I'm not here, and you're settling in for the night after a long day at work."

I've imagined what it would be like when I saw Owen again all day, but I didn't imagine it like this.

"So, you want to see me naked?" I ask playfully, attempting to ease my nerves.

Owen shrugs, keeping his expression bare. "If that's where a long day leads," he responds.

His words shouldn't excite me this much. I shouldn't want to comply, but I do.

I take my eyes off of Owen and pretend that he's not here.

I remove my pants first. Then pull my shirt over my head, letting it fall to the floor. I walk toward the bathroom in my bra and panties, pausing at the door before going inside. I want to ask Owen to join me, but he's not here. Instead, I leave the door open, hoping he'll stop by.

I draw myself a warm bath, finish getting undressed, pull my hair up into a bun, and sink into the water, lying my head against the bath pillow. My hand weaves through the bubbles above the water. Then, I rest my hand on the side of the bathtub and close my eyes.

I'm a little disappointed. My getting undressed wasn't the most romantic scene, and neither was my walk-away, but I thought Owen would be at least a tad bit interested in following me inside.

I glance at the opening to the bathroom, then turn back, closing my eyes again. I am relaxed, though, and maybe that was Owen's mission—to get me to relax and be myself even when he's around. The thought makes my heart grow fonder, and I smile, releasing a long breath.

"Mind if I join you?" Owen's voice pulls my eyes open a few seconds later.

I turn my head in his direction. He's blocking the door, leaning against the opening, watching me. His feet are bare, his arms crossed over his chest, and his eyes heated.

I'm not the least bit nervous. This relaxing thing is working. I feel like myself—confident and not hesitant to say what's on my mind.

"Not at all," I answered.

Owen draws his lower lip between his teeth and pushes off the wall. He stalks toward me, stopping inches away.

"So, you want to see me naked," Owen says, returning my words.

Yes. Yes, please.

I shrug indifferently. "Would be the perfect complement to my long day."

Owen bows his head and closes his eyes for a moment as if he's preparing himself. He opens his eyes and steps back a fraction, gripping the tale of his shirt and pulling it over his head. His eyes are on me, and I can't look away. He takes his time releasing the button on his jeans, unzipping, and pushing them down his thighs. Then, he steps out of them, pausing with his hands on the waistband of his boxers.

I grip the side of the bathtub while anticipating Owen's next move. My eyes venture down to the bulge beneath his waist. My mouth goes dry as he slides the material over his hips, and his dick springs forward. I move my eyes back to his, trying to appear normal—the opposite of what I feel.

Owen steps closer, his eyes glancing to my breast, then back to my eyes. "Back or front?" He asks.

It's such a simple question, but it's hard to decide. Either choice is risky, but I'd rather Owen stare at the back of my head than my face.

"Back," I decided, scooting forward for him to get behind me.

Owen settles into the bathtub and pulls me back against his chest. He's stoned against my lower back underwater, but I try to ignore it. I lay my head on Owen's right shoulder, and his arms circle my waist, hands flattening on my belly. I relax, feeling more at home with him here than I ever have.

"Tell me about your day," Owen says, nipping at my ear.

Owen told me that I wasn't ready, but I think that I am. The flush of heat radiating through my body says that I am. How can he expect me not to want him when he does things like this?

"Well, there's not much to tell. I saw four clients, two of which were new," I say, and Owen pulls my earlobe into his mouth, sucking softly. I clear my throat.

"What did you have for breakfast & lunch?" Owen asks, breathing down my neck.

"Coffee and a bagel for breakfast. A salad for lunch," I answered shakily.

"And your friends at work. Tell me about them," Owen says, placing a kiss on my shoulder. I breathe deeply, and his palm travels up my belly to cup my breast.

"That's a very short list," I tell him between breaths. "Maggie is probably the closest thing I have to a friend at work. She tried getting me to spill the beans about the roses, but...." I pause, sucking in a breath as Owen massages my nipple between his fingers.

"But," Owen inquires.

"I don't know. I guess I'm wary of people finding out—afraid of making the same mistakes I did before."

Owen releases my nipple, bringing his hand up to my face. He tilts my chin to look at him over my shoulder.

"I know that someone hurt you, Soph. I knew it the first time I ever saw you," Owen gives me a sad smile. "One day, when you're ready, I want you to tell me about it. But until then, be here with me and trust that I am not that guy. I am not here to cause you or Ellis harm. My goal is to please you—to show you how a real man treats his lady. To be deserving of everything that you have to give."

A mass of butterflies swarms my stomach, weakening me, then bringing me back to life again.

Owen's lips slide across mine, then he kisses me delicately, slowly before pulling away.

I turn away from him, looking at the wall in front of us with my mind racing in every direction.

I want to tell Owen everything. I want to look into his eyes with no secrets between us. I want to touch him with clean hands and a clean heart. I want to be ready in every sense of the word. I want to fall in love with him and know that he loves all of me back, even the broken parts.

One day.

"I'm going to try something, Soph," Owen says, trailing his fingers down my side. "If you want me to stop, say the word."

I nod, and Owen's hand moves over my thigh, then between my legs. His palm curves over my center as his thumb strums my pulsing bud. He slips two fingers inside of me, and I moan softly, pressing my head against his shoulder. His fingers begin to coast in and out of me as his thumb flicks down and up. He teases my breast with his other hand, his fingers circling my nipple. His lips are pressed against my back, and his warm breath covers my neck.

I rock my hips onto his fingers, loving the way he makes me feel. I've never had this, never had a man worship my body the way Owen does. His actions are perfect, professional, yet personal at the same time. His movements are so fluid like a song played from memory.

"Melody," Owen whispers next to my ear. "Sweet, sweet, Melody." His hard shaft pulses at my back as he continues.

It's torturous what he's doing to himself.

And pure pleasure, what he's doing to me.

"Oh. My. Owen," I say breathlessly. My eyes pop open. Then I clamp them shut. A sensation that I've never felt before overtakes me. I dig my nails into Owen's thighs, and he strums faster, his fingers pumping harder inside of me.

"You're almost there. Don't hold back, Soph," Owen says.

Almost there. Almost where?

I can barely think through the fog in my head, but I can't stop what's happening. I don't want him to stop. I keep moving against his fingers. He keeps moving his fingers into me. Something inside of me clenches, and my body begins to quake.

"That's it," I barely hear Owen say, flattening his other hand over my belly.

My moan comes louder, and Owen holds me, guiding me safely over the edge. My fingers loosen on his thighs, and I collapse against his body, sated and out of breath.

Owen grabs my hand and brings it to his lips, holding it there for a few seconds afterward. I don't understand how he's so hard against my back and still so calm and attentive to me.

What Owen did, deserves a thank you or an award, but that would be weird. So, I try for a little truth.

"No one has ever done that before," I say.

Owen's chuckle vibrates through me. "What? Pleasure you in the bathtub?"

"No. Yes. I mean. I've heard stories about the big O, but I've never experienced anything quite like this. I've never had an orgasm," I say, looking over my shoulder.

The smile drops from Owen's face. "Well, I'm honored to be the first to give it to you," he says, seriously, bringing his face close to mine. "And it won't be the last," he adds before kissing me.

Nine

Owen

Sophia and I have spent the last month talking, learning, and falling more for each other. We haven't spent every day together, but we've talked every night and kept our promise to see each other more often. I'm convinced now more than ever that Sophia was meant for me.

Sophia thinks that it's time we talk with Ellis. So, I'm going to her place once she's home from work. I'm ready for the next step, but there's one thing weighing on me. What if Ellis doesn't accept me as the man in his mother's life? I've spent a few fleeting moments with him this past week as uncle Dalton's friend, so he knows me. He even likes me, but all of that could be thrown out the window after he learns the whole truth. Sophia and I going public will change Ellis' life forever.

It's probably not fair to spring this on Ellis with me leaving in a few days for our next show, but I also think the timing couldn't be better. It will give him time to process the fact and Sophia time to help him through it while I'm gone.

I walk into my parents' home, following the sound of running water into the kitchen. The water shuts off when I turn the corner. Mom is standing at the sink, rubbing her hands with a dry cloth. She turns around as I enter, smiling brightly.

"Owen," she says as I walk over to her and kiss her cheek.

"Hey, Mom."

My mom and I have gotten a lot closer since I've been home. Dad is still himself. I communicate with them better than before, but they still seem hesitant. It's as if they're keeping the last ten percent of closeness guarded and out of my reach. I guess it's a plus that they don't look at me with disappointment anymore. It's more like fear now, and I can't figure out why that is.

"I want to talk to you about something," I tell her, backing up to the counter behind me. I've thought long and hard about this, and I think it's time that she knew about Sophia.

"Okay," Mom says, leaning her back against the counter in front of me. She puts the rag down and crosses her arms over her chest. "Talk."

We've never talked much about girls before, aside from asking me if I had a girlfriend and whether I was safe. My answer was always *no* and *yes*. I bunch my brows, unsure of how mom will react.

"I've met someone, and things are getting serious," I admit.

Mom raised an eyebrow, shuffling from one foot to the other. "I figured there was a reason you were gone half the time," Mom says. "So, what's her name? What's she like?" She questions.

"Her name is Sophia. She's Dalton's younger sister."

Mom stares at me for a long moment, her smile fading. Her eyes crinkled at the corners. "Are you sure that's the best idea?" She asks. "You boys have been friends for so long. Are you sure you want to risk that?"

It doesn't matter if I'm sure or not. "It's already done," I say. "Dalton and I talked about it. He's on board, and I really like her."

"And are you ready to take on the role of a father figure?" Mom asks. "It's a huge responsibility, Owen."

Mom knows all about Ellis from the headlines years ago. She probably thinks I'm out of my mind, but my mind is as clear as it's ever been.

"I'm ready to try," I answered truthfully. "I know that you think I'm too young, that I shouldn't get involved," I sigh. "But of all the women I've met, Sophia is the only one that makes me feel something real. And her son is a bonus. I adore him."

Mom is quiet for a long moment before she smiles half-heartedly. She leans forward, placing her hand over my heart. "You've always had a big heart, Owen. I admire that about you, but people can be cruel, son. Just be sure that this," Mom says, patting my chest and dropping her hand, "is spent on the right one."

I nod because I believe my heart is in the right place with Sophia. I can't imagine her hurting me.

"I want you to meet her when I'm back from the next show," I say.

"That serious, huh," Mom says, clearing her throat. "If that's what you want, I would love to meet her." She touches my arm. Then drops her hand to her side, and a dismal smile curves her lips.

"Thanks, Mom." I pushed off of the counter and began walking toward the exit.

Mom whispers behind me, but I hear it plain as day. "I have to warn him."

I almost stop to ask who she's talking about, but I have to meet Sophia. Maybe she's talking about Dad. He's always hated the attention that came along with my profession. I shrug it off and keep walking, focusing on the next task at hand.

"Am I too early?" I ask Sophia as I step inside her home.
"No, come on in. Ellis is outside in the backyard."

I step close to her, joining her pinky with mine. "I'm going to miss you," I tell her, staring into her eyes.

"I'm not going anywhere. Ellis will be fine with us. You'll see."

"I'm talking about the show. I won't see you for two weeks," I say, flicking Sophia's chin.

Sophia grins. "I'll miss you too," she says, tipping up and placing a chaste kiss on my lips. "But we can still talk and text. And we'll both be up to our neck in distraction otherwise. So, we'll get through it," she tries to convince me.

I glance at the back door, then back at Sophia. "Are you sure you don't want to wait until I get back?" I ask her.

"Yes," Sophia gently touches my cheek. "Why don't you get comfortable while I go get him."

I pull her in for a quick kiss before she disappears. Then I sit on the couch and wait. Three minutes felt more like three hours while Sophia was gone. Uncertainty tries to steal my attention, but I shove it away.

"Owen," Ellis says with a mix of excitement and confusion.

It's the first time Ellis and I have been in his domain together, and while I know this place like the back of my hand now, I pretend that I'm just visiting.

"Hey, Bud," I say, pounding his fist with mine.

Sophia sits a few feet away from me and pats the spot between us. "Sit down, Baby," she instructs Ellis. "I—We have something to tell you."

Ellis sits, glancing at me, then Sophia. Sophia covers his hand with hers, giving him the sweetest motherly smile. It's much different than the smile she has stored for me, and I love this one just as much.

"Do you know what it means when two people are dating?" Sophia asks Ellis.

Ellis scrunches his nose in thought. "Like Uncle Dalton and Auntie Jos?"

I smile at that.

"Uncle Dalton is married, so it's a little different. They have learned so much about each other and love each other so much that they decided to live together forever. When two people are dating, they are still learning. They like each other. They don't live together yet, but they hope that one day they will." Sophia explains, glancing at me for a moment.

I give her an encouraging smile. I couldn't have explained it better if I had tried.

Ellis glances at me for a few seconds before returning his attention to his mom. "Like you and Owen?" he asks.

Sophia blinks at his question, shock flashing briefly across her face. When her expression returns to normal, she says, "Yes, like Owen and me. We're really good friends, and he's going to be spending a lot more time here if you're okay with it."

I watch Ellis, wondering what's going through his head. I don't want to think about losing them if he's not cool with us being together.

Ellis looks up at me, his gaze questioning, and I prepare myself for whatever he has to say.

"Are you going to be my dad?" Ellis asks.

I cough, a chuckle spilling free. I wasn't expecting that, so I don't know how to answer. Of course, I would love for Ellis to call me dad one day, but that's not my decision to make. I answer the best way that I know how to.

"I don't know, Bud, but I would love to spend some more time with you. If that's okay."

Ellis doesn't respond, and I noticed that he does that when he's thinking—like Sophia covering her mouth when she's nervous. "Can I go back outside for a little while?" He asks.

Sophia's mouth twitches. "Sure, Baby."

Ellis stands, walking fast toward the door. He pauses with the door open. "Can Owen come with me?"

Sophia looks at me for confirmation, and I let out a long breath of relief. "Right behind you, Bud," I tell him.

Ellis takes off running without a backward glance. Sophia and I both chuckled before I stood. I press my lips against her temple. Then join Ellis outside.

Ellis is just a kid, but he's a smart kid. So, I know that this is his way of accepting me, and in doing so, he's also testing me. I will not fail him or Sophia.

• • • • ♪ ♪ • • • • •

"How would you feel about meeting my mother?" I asked Sophia later that night.

Sophia's eyes shoot up to mine from where her head lay across my lap. It's just past nine, and Ellis just fell asleep in his bed.

"Honestly?" Sophia asks, and I nod. She looks away bleakly. "I don't know," she answered, scrunching her forehead.

"It's not a proposal, Soph." *Not yet.* "I just want you to meet the other woman in my life," I explained.

Sophia takes a deep breath. "I guess that would be okay." She fiddles with her fingers over her belly. "Does she know about Ellis? That I have a son?" She asks nervously.

"She does." I brush my thumb over her cheek. "If it makes you feel any better, I've already spoken to her about it."

Sophia sits up, turning to face me. "You spoke to your mother about me?"

"Yes, and she wants to meet you when I get back. No pressure."

"Does any of this scare you?" Sophia questions, throwing me off.

Up until this moment, her nervousness seemed to have wilted away.

"No," I say simply. "Are you having second thoughts? Think we're moving too fast?"

"No, that's not it." Sophia places her hand in mine. "We've been together for nearly two months. I think everything is falling into place. But that's what unnerves me." She gives my hand a gentle squeeze. "I'm probably breaking some sort of code telling you this, but you're the perfect guy, Owen. And you've done everything right. But I'm not so perfect. I've done things that I'm not proud of," she admits. A cloud forms in her eyes, and her lids close over them.

I want to know what's causing her pain, but I don't want to pry. I believe she will tell me in her own time.

"Hey," I say, pulling her into my arms. "None of us are perfect, certainly not me," I say reassuringly. "I just know that I want you in my life, and whatever storms may come, we'll face them together. I'm not easily frightened away. You have to know that by now."

"I do, but…."

"No buts," I object. I tilt Sophia's chin up so that she's staring into my eyes. "It's me, you, and Ellis against all odds. Nothing is going to change that," I declare.

Sophia straddles me, her arms wrapping loosely around my neck. I grip her waist as her hips grind slowly on top of me. I tilt my head, touching my lips to hers in a sweet kiss that quickly turns torturous. I'm tempted to take her to bed and strip her naked, but I can't. I said I'd wait until she was ready.

Sophia thinks I'm a saint for holding out this long, giving her all the pleasure while I suffer inside. Anyone else would probably call me a fool. I have many times, but Sophia is worth every cold shower and lonely night. She's worth the wait.

I pull away from Sophia's lips, and our eyes meet. As I stare into her eyes, I know that if she were to tease just a little bit harder, or if a plea falls from her lips, I won't be able to resist her tonight. I'm high on something foreign that feels so good, and as hard as I'm trying to come down, it's not working.

"Owen," Sophia whispers. "I'm ready. I need to feel *you*," she says pointedly, teasing the hair at the back of my neck with her fingers.

"What about Ellis," I allude.

"Ellis sleeps like a log, and I'll be as quiet as a mouse," Sophia says. "I need something to hold on to while you're gone."

My dick strains against my jeans, begging to be released. It's hard to say no to an offer like that. I grip her ass, jerking her hips forward. "If we do this, I may never want to leave," I admit.

Sophia's mouth descends on mine, hot and heavy, and I'm unable to pull away. I wonder if it's possible to taste a feeling because I can taste it—how she will feel finally wrapped around me, the warmth, and smooth friction. I can taste the rhythm of our movements, sweet like glazed honey.

I wrap my arm around her back, giving in to temptation. "Hold on tight, Melody," I whisper in Sophia's ear. Then I stand, taking her with me. She wraps her legs around me. Her thighs pressed firmly against my sides as I walked us to her bedroom.

Sophia releases her grip on me, planting her feet on the floor. She helps me undress, and I do the same for her, discarding every inch of fabric from our bodies.

"Let's make a memory," Sophia says, running her palm down my chest.

I edge closer, and Sophia creeps backward until the back of her knees hits the bed, and she falls back onto it with her knees up and legs together.

I run my hands over her legs, coaxing them open. "Don't be shy, Soph," I smirk.

The room is dark aside from the moonlight shining through the window, but I can see clearly as if the light were blazing bright. Sophia is beautiful inside and out.

Sophia scoots further onto the bed, and I climb in after her. I dip my head between her thighs, lapping at her smooth center once, twice, and again before dipping my tongue inside of her. Her back arches, and my dick throbs at her reaction.

"Please, Owen," Sophia begs.

I rise to my knees and press my thumb firmly against her clit before moving in a circular motion.

"Owen, I need you," Sophia says. "Now." She pulls me down, and I brace myself on my elbows to keep from collapsing on top of her.

I brush against her fold, holding on to what little restraint I still possess. Her arousal coats my shaft, warm and inviting, but I don't want to rush this. If we're making a memory, I want it to be lasting.

I kiss her shoulder, then pepper her neck with my lips, allowing my tongue to slip out to taste her skin. I suck gently at the base of her neck, and Sophia tilts her head to one side, allowing full access. She reaches between us, filling her hands with my shaft.

A low growl escapes me as her hands begin to move over me. I bury my face into her neck, enjoying the sensation. I need her just as much as she needs me. I can't hold back any longer.

I reach down, grabbing Sophia's hand and moving it above her head. Her heated gaze strikes me, setting fire to my desire.

It's been a while since I've been inside a woman. Even then, none of them came close to what I feel now. I've only sampled the exterior of Sophia's glory and already feel like I'm nearing the end. We're climbing an enticingly dangerous slope, and I want to reach the top without consequence.

"Soph, wait," I say, lifting off of her.

Sophia frowns, her eyebrows turning down with it. "Is something wrong?"

"Everything is exactly right," I tell her.

I reach down on the floor for my pants, digging into my pocket for my wallet. I open it up, remove the condom inside, and drop my pants and wallet on the floor. I kneel before Sophia, carefully opening the wrapper. It's my only one, and I'll be damned if this ends now.

"Want to do the honors?" I ask Sophia.

"Yes," Sophia nods, pulling her bottom lip into her mouth. She takes the condom from my hand, and I watch closely as she rolls it onto me with focus and precision.

When she's done, I position myself at her center, pausing for a long moment. I brush my finger over her forehead, pushing her hair behind her ear.

"You're so fucking cute, Soph," I say before easing inside of her.

Sophia's eyes close on a gasp, and I press my lips to hers. She kisses me back, and the pressure from her thighs gives way to my sides.

I entwine our fingers over her head while cupping her breast with my other hand. I pull her nipple into my mouth, grinding into her, and Sophia moans loudly, breaking her agreement. It's music to my ears, but I don't want to risk waking Ellis. I cover her mouth with mine to muffle the sound, and her voice vibrates, shaking me to my core.

I pull away from her lips, looking down at her smooth, blushed skin, then into her eyes. "Sweet, sweet, Melody," I murmur, pushing harder, faster into her.

Sophia's hand tightens in mine, and she grips the back of my thigh with her other hand. Her nails bite my skin as she urges me forward with every thrust of my hips.

Warmth and pleasure build inside of me, and I fight it, holding it captive until Sophia reaches her climax. I want this memory to be complete for both of us.

"Yes," Sophia whisper-shouts. "Yes." Her head tilts back, pressing into the pillow as her back arched off the bed. She contracts around me, her body shuddering uncontrollably.

Sophia relaxed onto the bed, breathing heavily after a few seconds, and I finally let go, pounding into her. My dick spasms, and my hips jerk. My entire body stiffens, and my vision blurs for a long moment. "Fuck," I say quietly, riding the wave.

I needed this.

I needed her.

I brace myself for a moment before moving to lie next to Sophia. I kiss her shoulder, then get up and walk to the bathroom, discarding the condom in the small trash bin beside the countertop.

I'm standing there staring into my own eyes through the mirror when Sophia walks up behind me. Her arms circle my waist, and she places her forehead on the center of my back.

Getting to know Sophia was the smartest decision I've ever made. She keeps surprising me without realizing it. Until her, my thoughts have been coherent, straight-lined. And now they're a jagged rush of everything.

I've been falling for Sophia slowly, carefully, but I didn't expect this. I didn't expect my heart to feel like it was beating out of my chest. I didn't expect to feel as if my world is now complete and to have a fear of losing it all at once.

I take a deep breath, closing and opening my eyes. I unclasp Sophia's hand from my waist and turn to face her. She stares up at me, smiling, and I cup my hands to her cheeks. She's the happiest I've ever seen her, and the hesitance that she'd shown in the beginning is nowhere to be found.

It's what I wanted, to have Sophia see me as more than just a brand. To be able to touch her without her flinching away. I've never felt this way for anyone before, and as frightened as I am, it suits me. I'm never letting this go.

"I love you, Soph," I say around the lump in my throat. "I'm fucking terrified, but I love you," I say truthfully.

Sophia's smile falters, and she swallows my truth. I almost expect her to run or object, but she doesn't. She continues to hold my stare. I don't expect her to say it back, not until she's ready. I just needed her to know where I stood.

I lower my head, placing my lips on hers in a sweet, meaningful kiss. Then, I touch my forehead to hers. I drop my hands to her waist, pulling her closer to me. A long moment passes as we stand there naked and uncaring. Then, we wash up and go to bed because there's no way I'm leaving her tonight.

Ten

Sophia

Rose sings, "Girl's night," as soon as I opened my front door. Both of her hands hold a bottle of wine, which makes me laugh.

The boys are spending the night with Dalton's mom, so we have the place to ourselves.

Owen has been away with the band for the past ten days, and I've been trying not to miss him. I didn't think him being in a different area code would be this hard. I've never asked, but I wonder if it's hard on Rose and Joselyn too.

I step aside, and Rose walks past me, followed by Joselyn and Katie. It's been a while since we've hung out like this, and it's because of Rose that we're here together now.

I close the door behind me and follow them into the living room. I sit on the couch and pull my legs up onto it. Joselyn sits on the floor next to me, and Katie takes the recliner.

"First rule of girl's night," Rose announces, standing before us. "No talking about men. Second rule, no thinking about men. Third rule, drink and be merry."

Laughter erupts from us, and Rose joins in.

"Excuse me," Katie inquires, gaining our attention. "If we can't talk about men and can't think about men, then what's left?" She asks.

"Duh," Rose mocks. "Third rule," she says, raising the bottles high above her head.

Between the four of us, the bottles are empty within an hour, and we're all strewn about on the floor. I didn't drink much, but a little is all it takes for me to feel woozy. Joselyn barely drank at all.

I turn onto my side, bracing my chin in one hand while my other palm is flat on the floor, steadying me. Since we started drinking, we haven't mentioned one man's name, and I'm about to break that streak.

"Owen wants me to meet his mother," I say aloud.

Joselyn looks at me, widening her eyes, but she doesn't speak right away.

On the other hand, Rose sits up, resting her back on the bottom of the couch across from me. "I was wondering who would be the first to break," she says. "Men. Why are they so consuming?" She questions. However, I'm not sure if she's asking for herself or me.

Joselyn ignores Rose's comment. "Is that what you want?" She asks me from the spot next to Rose.

I shrug. "I guess so. No. I don't know. Yes," I decided. "I want a life with Owen. I'm certain of that, but the thought of meeting his mother makes me nervous. He said that it's not a big deal, but everyone knows what a step like this means," I sigh. "I haven't even told him that I…." I pause, not wanting the words to be in vain the first time I say them.

"You didn't have to tell him," Rose says, reading between the lines. "Owen is one of the most perceptive men that I know. Reminds me of myself," she grins. "Trust me. He already knows."

"What's really bothering you, Sophia?" Joselyn asks.

My eyes snap to hers. "What if Owen's mother doesn't like me?"

"What if she doesn't?" Rose shrugs. "It's not going to change what Owen feels for you. The only one who can do that is you," she tells me.

"She's right, you know," Joselyn agrees. "Of course, it would be nice to have the stars align perfectly, but it wouldn't be a deal-breaker if she doesn't like you. Rose and I were where you are not long ago, and we got lucky. Maybe you will too."

I half-smile, half-nod, taking in their words. My buzz is wearing off talking about Owen, and a different kind of buzz is taking over. I miss him.

"How do you deal with the separation, the fame, the fans, any of it?" I ask. I may be a tad bit jealous of his groupies right now. I know that it's his job to entertain, but the thought of anyone else touching him and being so close annoys me. It also makes me realize how special I am that he chose me.

"Girl's night," Rose answers with a chuckle.

"I don't have that problem," Katie chimed in. She's been quiet most of the night, and I wonder if she feels left out now that I'm coupled with Owen.

Joselyn and I laugh.

"Well," Joselyn says. "This is going to sound hypocritical, but ignore the tabloids and magazines, unless it's Young & Common because we print the truth." She winks. "Keep the communication open between you and Owen. Feed your relationship. Spend time together away from everything and everyone. Build up a strong foundation of trust because you won't last without it. And of course, girl's night doesn't hurt either."

My phone rings on the table, and I reach up to grab it. Owen's name fills my screen, and my lips curve into a smile. I stand up, mouthing that I'd be back, and turn in the direction of my room.

"Hello," I answered without a second thought. I step inside my bedroom and close the door behind me.

"Soph," Owen says in a tone that shoots straight to my core.

He's called me every night since we've been apart, but it just doesn't compare. The calls never last long, and he's always in the middle of something. I plop down on the bed, looking up at the ceiling, wishing he were here in the flesh.

"How did it go tonight?" I ask.

"The usual. Large crowd. Ear bursting noise. Handsy fans." There's muffled noise in the background, but I try to focus on his voice and ignore his last statement. "I'm counting down the days until I'm back home," Owen says.

I'm counting down the days too.

"How is girl's night going?" Owen asks, catching me off guard.

"How did you know about that?"

"Married people," came his response. Owen chuckles on the other end of the line. "But it's all good. I hope you're enjoying yourself."

"I am. We are. It's nice hanging out with people my age," I grin. "You've changed my life, Owen Daye." And he has. Before him, I never would've let Ellis out of my sight. I didn't do clubs or make out with anyone I barely knew. I had no intention of falling in love, but I have.

The background noise goes from quiet to loud. A male voice calls Owen's name, and a few words are spoken that I can't make out. Then the noise quiets again.

"Sorry, Soph. I have to go. Time to appease the crowd," Owen says. "Dap Ellis for me. I love you."

"I love you too," I say before the line goes dead. I suck in a sharp breath. The words slipped out so effortlessly, shocking me. I don't even know if Owen heard them. I'm hoping that he didn't. I wanted to tell him face to face, at the right time—not blurted out like some plea of desperation while he's on tour.

I hang up the phone, staring at the screen, noting that it's nearly an hour before midnight. I grab a few blankets and pillows and walk back into the living room. Rose, Jos, and Katie quiet down when I walk into the room.

"Young love," Rose mocks, and I snicker at her comment.

I hand each of them a set and return to my spot on the floor, thinking it's going to be a long night. Hearing Owen's voice woke up every nerve in my body, and sleep was the furthest thing from my mind.

"Says the woman who's still in the honeymoon phase," I retort.

"And I intend to keep it that way." Rose wiggles her brows.

I chuckle under my breath, getting comfy on the floor.

After Owen's call last night, we couldn't get off the topic of men. It didn't matter if they were ours or not. And now

I'm about to be alone again, at least until Ellis comes home tonight.

"We have to do this again soon," Joselyn says on her way out the door. Rose and Katie are halfway to the car.

"For sure," I agree.

I watch them get into the car. Then, I close the door thinking of what to do next. I plop down on the couch, still tired from the late night. I slept for four hours and was fine with it until now.

A measly yawn escapes me, and I tilt my head back on the couch, looking up at the ceiling. Seconds later, the doorbell rings, causing me to look in that direction. I blow out a breath and plaster on a smile.

I swing open the door, thinking it's one of the ladies. "Okay, what did you leave?" I ask, but there's no one there, and Joselyn's car is gone. I step outside, looking from one corner of the house to the other.

"Now you're imagining things," I tell myself. I shake it off and go back inside. "You should get some sleep," I say into the air.

This time I keep walking toward my bedroom. I lay on top of the covers and pull them over me, closing my eyes.

Eleven

Owen

I'm attuned to everything now, far more than before. The cement is firm beneath my feet. The calm air and brutal heat bathe my skin. But I welcome it because it means that I'm home. It means that Sophia will soon be within arm's reach. I can't think of a better way to spend my Saturday.

I asked Frank to bring me straight to Sophia's house from the plane. We moved up our flight time from tonight, so she has no clue that I'm here.

Sophia blurted that she loved me over the phone days ago and hasn't repeated those words since. I haven't been able to forget them. I'm wondering if it was my imagination.

I ring the doorbell, then anxiously rub the back of my neck, waiting.

The door swings open moments later. The joyous surprised look on Sophia's face was just what I'd expected.

"Owen, you're here," Sophia says, shocked. Her hands fly up to palm her head. "I thought that I had more time," she adds.

I smirk at her nervous energy and step forward. My arm goes around her back, and I pull her to me. Sophia sucks in a sharp breath, her eyes widening. Then I kissed her. Her rigid body melts, folding onto me as she kisses me back. The past two weeks swarm between us like a live entity.

Sophia had the right idea, sending me off with a reminder of us, but now that I'm back, I just want more.

It takes me a moment to remember where we are. I loosen my grip on Sophia's waist and pull away from her lips, touching my forehead to hers.

"I've been waiting too long to taste your lips, Soph."

Sophia's tongue slips out, coating her skin. "Was it everything you'd hoped?"

"Even better. I'm going to need a lot more of that." I kiss the tip of her nose. "A lot more," I repeat.

Sophia grins.

"I hope you don't mind that I brought a friend," I continued, tapping the strap of my guitar case over my shoulder. "I didn't want to leave her in the car."

Sophia glances down at my case and back up. "And a sexy friend at that," Sophia teases. "She's always welcome." She looks around me to where Frank is still waiting in the car.

I had forgotten he was even here.

"Are you staying or going?" Sophia asks.

"You tell me. Frank could come back later if you're free," I answer.

"Get in here." Sophia takes my hand, pulls me inside with her, and closes the door.

I chuckle. "I missed you too," I say as we walk further inside.

Sophia lets go of my hand, and I set my guitar down on the couch in the living room. I sent Frank a quick text telling him he could leave. I face Sophia, contemplating another kiss, when Ellis yells, "Owen!"

My head jerks in his direction, and a smile lights my face. I've missed him too. He was more accepting of me than I thought he'd be. It probably helped that he already knew me, and I spent time with him as well. I imagine he feels less threatened that I'll take his mom away. I meant what I said. I want the whole package.

"Hey, Bud," I say to Ellis, and he surprises me by throwing his arms around me. I glance at Sophia, and she shrugs, seemingly impressed.

When Ellis lets go, he asks, "Are you leaving again?"

My heart swells and aches at the same time. I still don't know much about Ellis' dad, only that he and Sophia split before Ellis was born. I think it's safe to ask about him now that we're all on the same page, but I'll save that for later when Sophia and I are alone.

"I'll be around for a few weeks," I answer. "But don't worry. I'll always come back," I promise.

I'm curious if Ellis has ever seen his dad, if he asks about him and what Sophia said if he did. Maybe that's why she's been so guarded with him. The less interaction he has with others, the fewer questions he'll have.

"Can you play video games with me?" Ellis asks with dough eyes.

I look at Sophia. It's her call to make. "Do you mind?" I ask.

A flash of disappointment crosses her features before she plasters on a smile. "Have fun," she says.

I look back to Ellis. "Go get it set up. I'll be right there."

"Yeah!" Ellis exclaims, running off to the playroom.

I turn to Sophia and wrap my arms around her. I kiss her temple, her nose, and her lips, leaving a lasting impression. Then, I pull away.

"I'll make this up to you. Promise," I say. I begin backing away. "I'm sure you can think of a few ideas while I'm gone," I smirk, then turn around and walk toward the playroom.

Two hours later, Ellis has effectively beat me at almost every round of Mortal Kombat. Sophia popped her head in a few times while Ellis and I played, but she didn't interrupt our heated battle.

I forcibly set the joystick down on the floor beside the bean bag chair because throwing it is not an option. *Fuck*, rang loudly in my head, but I kept it there because of Ellis. Outside, I shoot him a forced smile. I don't like losing, but he's just a kid. He doesn't deserve my wrath.

"Good game, Bud. How about we take a break and go check on your mom?"

"Okay," Ellis says happily.

We find Sophia in the kitchen finishing up a small platter of sandwiches and veggies. She looks me up and down and clears her throat before smiling down at Ellis.

"Lunchtime," she says.

Ellis doesn't look surprised at all. He grabs two cups, pausing to look at me. Then, he reaches for another one and walks toward the table.

"Ellis, let's change things up today. Take them into the living room. We're having a slumber lunch," Sophia announces.

I raise an eyebrow. "Slumber lunch?" I asked.

Sophia shrugs, passing the tray to me. "Just go with it. Trust me," she says.

We followed Ellis to the living room, and I set the tray down in front of the comfy spot we picked on the floor. Sophia sits between Ellis and me. Ellis wanted to watch Transformers and Sophia agreed. The movie didn't matter to me, as long as I was here with them.

We eat while reacting to the television, and Ellis falls asleep near the movie's end with his head resting on Sophia's lap.

Sophia looks at me and smiles. "He takes a nap after lunch," Sophia whispers. "I'm not sure how long it will last once he starts school, so I'm enjoying it while it lasts."

I bring her hand to my lips for a few seconds, holding her gaze.

"Thank you," I say.

Sophia snickers. "For putting Ellis to sleep?" she asks.

"For taking a chance on me," I say. "You and Ellis, you make me better. You make me want more." I pause, brushing my thumb over her cheek. "Because of you, I can stop dreaming and start living." I take her hand in mine. "I wish you could feel what my heart feels when I'm with you."

Sophia's smile falters as she swallows hard. Her eyes gloss over as she stares at me. "I love you, Owen," she says shakily. "None of this seems real."

"It's very real, Soph, but maybe getting out of our bubble will help. Are you ready for that?" I ask.

Rumors are starting to circulate about Sophia and me, but I haven't confirmed or denied my involvement with her. I was hoping we would do that together, silently but publicly.

"What do you have in mind?" Sophia counters.

"Dinner and a movie," I shrug. "I've always wanted to get dirty in the back of a theater." I wiggle my eyebrows, and Sophia giggles quietly.

"Look at you with a wild side," Sophia mocks.

"Only for you."

"In that case, I'm ready for the world."

I tilt my head toward her, and Sophia leans closer. Our lips are a hair away when Ellis squirms. We let out a hushed laugh when he settled again. Then, I press my lips to hers.

Twelve

Sophia

Four days ago, I made yet another commitment to Owen. Tomorrow I will make good on that commitment, but there's something that I have to do first.

My stomach is in knots as I make the drive to my mom's house. It's an all too familiar feeling whenever I'm headed in this direction—one that I've never gotten used to. It's hard to forget about a past that lingers so heavily in the present.

There's a huge pain in my head when I think of Kenneth and an even bigger ache when I think of Ellis missing out on a father because Kenneth is a coward. In the end, I think Ellis will be better because of it.

I glance at Ellis in the back seat, tightening my fingers on the steering wheel. I don't know if Kenneth still lives in Brayberry or not, but he's the last person I want to run into. I left shortly after we split up, and it wasn't pretty or easy.

I met Kenneth in college, and like a good thief, he captured my heart. He was kind, dreamy, and attentive. He protected me and made me feel safe. I wish I had paid closer attention to the signs. The last time I saw him, he told me I was a piece of shit that didn't deserve the air I breathed.

Leaving was hard but necessary. My mother convinced me that a fresh start would be good for me, and my wayward father helped me get out. I didn't know my father well, but at least he felt something for me. He had a warped way of showing it, but he cared enough to keep me safe, and I never went without anything due to his generous donations. That's how I ended up in Cane.

"Are we almost there, Mom?" Ellis asks, peering at me through the rearview mirror.

"Almost." I manage a smile, then revert my attention to the highway. I pass the turnoff to what I remember to be Kenneth's old house, pressing the gas pedal a little harder. Anger and fear course through me, and I silently count to myself. It's sixty seconds between that turn and the stoplight leading to my mom's house, and it seems like the longest seconds of my life each time I pass. Somehow, making the turn off the main road makes everything better. It takes some of my anxiety away.

Five more minutes pass until we reach the home where I grew up. I park the car and blow out a long breath.

"We're here, Baby," I say to Ellis. "Let's go inside."

We get out of the car, and Ellis makes a beeline to the front door. Mom is expecting us, so I use my key to open the door. The smell of pancakes and coffee tickles my nose as we walk inside.

"Grandma, Grandma!" Ellis yells when he sees my mom coming toward us. He runs to her, and as big as he is, Mom scoops him up and twirls him around.

"It's my favorite grandson," Mom says.

"He's your only grandson," I reply, catching up to them. Mom and I both grin, and she sets Ellis down.

"Grandma, where's Jinx?" Ellis asks about Mom's Pomeranian dog.

Ellis and Jinx are tight as a whip, but I think he hates me with the snotty looks he gives me. We've come to an understanding over the years. I won't bother him if he doesn't bother me.

"He's in the backyard. Go on out if you want. He'll be happy to see you," Mom says.

Ellis looks at me for approval. "Can I, Mom?"

"Go," I nod. I need to talk to Mom alone anyway. It will give us some time.

Ellis hurries off, and Mom turns to me when he's out of sight.

"So, you said you had something to discuss," Mom jumps straight to the point, and I follow suit.

"I've met someone." I sit down on one of the barstools at the bar, and Mom sits next to me.

"So, the rumors are true," Mom states more than asks. "Owen, is it?" She rests her elbow on the countertop, flattening her palm. "The guitar player."

"Yes. I just wanted you to hear officially from me first."

"Are you sure that's the best thing for you and Ellis?" Mom asks, wrinkling her forehead. "Is your safety no longer a priority?"

"That's the thing, I've convinced myself for so long that I wasn't safe to the point where I believed it—still believe it. Maybe it's time that I get over that fear and start living a normal life again."

Mom tilts her head, giving me a sorrowful smile. "It's easier said than done, Sophia." Mom grabs my hand, giving it a gentle squeeze. "But, if anyone can, it's you. You are stronger than your fiercest enemy, and you deserve to be happy." Mom Sighs. "I will say that it's been a long time since I've seen that gleam in your eyes."

My smile widens. "What I feel for Owen is indescribable. For the first time in my life, I care about what I want. I'm finding myself again, and I credit Owen for a lot of the why."

"Have you told him about Kenneth?" Mom asks. "Because at the rate you're going, the truth will surface," She warns.

"I haven't, and Owen hasn't asked much of me. He's so patient, and things have been great. I didn't want to ruin his perception of me, but I will tell him. I have no choice."

Mom squinted her eyes. "Don't do that," she says, looking straight through me. "What happened between you and Kenneth is not your fault. Don't blame yourself for his stupidity. Do you hear me?"

"I know, and I don't. Not anymore. Not entirely. But Owen," I pause, glancing away for a few seconds and back.

"If Owen is the man that you think he is, he will understand. Besides, he probably had more than a few nuts in his basket." Mom taps my thigh.

Mom is right. Owen will understand, but will he still see me the same way? I swallow the thought, attempting to bury it deep inside of me.

"Thanks, Mom." I reach over and pull her in for a hug.

"Don't thank me yet," Mom says as I release her. She grabs my hand. "I suspect you'll bring Owen to meet me soon," Mom inquires.

I'm stumped for a moment on how to respond. I'm closer with my mom now because I've learned to accept the truth, but I don't know how Owen would feel about meeting her. Mrs. Evers is like a second mother to him, and she and I are close too. Despite her husband's actions, she welcomed me into her life without a second thought. Regardless, Owen may feel like he's betraying her in some way.

Instead of writing off the idea, I say, "Soon." I'll speak to Owen about it.

"Good. Now, let's go rescue Jinx." Mom laughs and stands. I stand too and follow her outside.

Ellis, Mom, and I spend the rest of the day together. After Ellis falls asleep in the guest room, I retire to my childhood bedroom for the night.

I lie awake for hours staring at the ceiling, tossing and turning. An uneasy feeling settled in my stomach, and I felt the need to hurl, but the bile was stuck in my throat. I know that seeing Kenneth again is probably inevitable, but I don't like being this close. I feel as if he could pop up at any minute, and I'd rather not be surprised.

I huff out a frustrated breath, blinking into the moonlit room.

"What would you do if he showed up?" I whisper.

"How would you explain that to Ellis?"

Ellis is beginning to ask questions about his dad. The latter is a question I've asked myself over the years but never found an answer for. Instead of disclosing the absolute truth, I've been bending it, responding that, *"I don't know where he is, Baby,"* because the truth seems like the biggest lie of all.

The concept of Ellis hating me mingles with my unrest. I grab a pillow and put it to my face, screaming into it. Then, I let it fall onto my belly.

The only way out of this mess is through it.

The thought brings Owen to my mind. And the notion of Owen eases my nausea. So, I keep him there and close my eyes, forcing all other ideas away.

Thirteen

Owen

I glance at Sophia in the back passenger seat. "How was the visit with your mom?"

Frank pretends that he's not listening from the driver's seat.

Sophia has been quiet all day. I'm not sure if the visit with her mom is the cause or our public date night tonight. I refrained from asking her, but now I'm beginning to worry.

Sophia glances at me, forcing a smile. Her fingers draw imaginary circles on her left knee. "It was nice spending time with her." Sophia wrinkles her brows and looks forward. The way she's behaving reminds me of the Sophia I first met.

"So, what are you not telling me? Why the long face?"

"Mom wants to meet you," Sophia says, still not making eye contact.

"Easy. Let's make it happen." I smile, but Sophia doesn't look happy. I cover her hand with mine on her leg. "Did something else happen?"

Sophia's fingers latch onto mine. "There's something you should know, Owen." She offers a sullen smile. "But not now. Can we just enjoy tonight?"

I nod. "Whatever you want."

We arrive at the theater a few minutes later, and Frank pulls up to the front door. The parking lot is nearly bare as I had intended. We're early, and the first movie doesn't start for another hour.

I pull the hood of my short-sleeved shirt over my head, and Sophia does the same with hers. The vibes she's giving off in my oversized hoodie are fucking sexy. I stare at her for a moment, rethinking this whole thing, not because I don't want to be here with her. I would rather be inside of her instead.

I thought it was a good idea to try and dim our presence while here, but I didn't know it would affect me like this.

"Ready?" Sophia squeezes my hand, jarring me from my thoughts.

More than ready.

"Yeah, let's do it," I responded.

I called ahead and spoke with the manager, and she agreed to give us early access. She doesn't want a riot at her theater any more than I do.

A young man opens the door for us, locking it after Sophia and I enter. None of the employees look surprised, but I do sense a few fans who, I'm guessing, are forbidden to react. I already know that leaving won't be as easy as our arrival by the looks on their faces.

I hold Sophia's hand until we settle in the back of an empty room. They keep the lights low as instructed, for now, giving us limited privacy for the next twenty minutes.

"So, we wait," Sophia says into the darkness.

What I said days ago popped into my head. "We could make use of the time and create a preview of our own," I suggest.

Sophia grins, covering her mouth with her hand until realization dawns. Her expression changes. "You're serious."

My eyes flick to her lips, and I trace them with my thumb. "I want to do wicked things with you, Soph. I want to polish your thighs with my hips."

"Right now?" She says breathily.

"What better time than now?"

Sophia looks around the room nervously, but I can tell she wants it just as much, if not more.

"Someone might see us."

I lean close to her ear, trailing the tip of my nose down the length of her lobe. "We'll be quick and quiet. And when I get you home, we'll finish the movie." I cup her jaw with my fingers, turning her head to face me. "Do you trust me?"

Sophia's breathing picks up, brushing against my lips. "Yes."

I close the distance between us, pressing my lips to hers. Our mouths part and I tilt my head for better access. Our tongues twist and mingle, and my dick springs to life, rising toward the elastic of my shorts.

"Sophia pulls away from my lips, gasping for air. "Owen."

I release my dick from its cell, stroking it within my palm. "Pull down your pants and panties, and come sit on it. I'm taking you for a ride."

Sophia looks around, hesitant once more. Then, she does as I said, freeing herself completely. I pull out a condom, sheathing myself. She stands before me, facing the big screen, and I slip my hand between her thighs from behind. I slowly finger the length of her fold, and she whimpers.

"Quiet, Soph." I pull my bottom lip into my mouth to hold in my excitement. Her skin is smooth, warm, and, "So fucking wet," I ground out. I slip two fingers inside of her, then bring them to my mouth to taste her. "And sweet."

I grip Sophia's hips, guiding her down onto me, and she conforms to me like a glove. My left arm goes around her belly as she begins to move. My other hand travels to the swollen bud between her thighs, teasing and urging her on. She grips the arms of the chair, and the whole row trembles.

"Melody," I say against the base of her neck.

Sophia continues her assault, and each time she falls, I rise to meet her thrust for thrust. Her head leans back, and a gush of air leaves her. I press my forehead to her spine and my palm to her belly, flicking my thumb over her clit. "Let go for me, Soph."

"Owen, I'm…." Sophia's words trail off, her movement slowing as she tightens around me, nails digging into the leather armrest.

I pound into her, and her head goes slack on my shoulder, body quivering over me. I rocket into her again, and again, and again, until I find my release.

I groan into her neck, peppering kisses there, giving us both a minute to come down. I don't want her to move yet, but the lights will be on soon, and people will fill the space.

"Soph," I whisper, and she turns her head toward me so that we're facing each other. She kisses me, simply and sweetly. Then, she stands and composes herself.

I remove the condom, knotting it, and Sophia pulls a washcloth out of her purse.

"Were you expecting something?" I ask.

"I'm a mom," Sophia winks. "Always prepared for anything." She wipes me off, then secures the condom in the rag, returning it to her purse. Then, she sprays perfume into the air.

A few minutes later, the room goes from dark to dim, and the big screen turns on. Sophia and I remain in our corner with our heads hung low until the room darkens again.

I hardly notice the movie with Sophia next to me. The memory of what we did is still fresh in my mind. We slip out with our hoods on before the ending credits while the room is still full. But as expected, there are a few eyes and whispers following us through the lobby.

A camera flashes as we exit the theater, and I give Sophia's hand a reassuring squeeze. We hurry to where Frank is waiting by the curb and get into the car. The camera flashes again, but the dark tint shields us from it.

"Ready for part two?" I ask Sophia.

"Will it be anything like part one?" The corners of her lips turn up, eyes glistening in the dark.

"I would love to have you laid bare on a table so that I can devour you, but not for the whole world to see."

Sophia looks at Frank, and I follow her gaze. I smirk, returning my attention to her. I thought I saw a smile from Frank, but I could never be sure with him. Even if he were paying attention, I would never hear of this again. Our bodyguards are so good with discretion.

Sophia clears her throat. "Oh."

I put my arm around her, pulling her closer. "Part two is more subtle, more public, more cameras, but still intimate," I continued.

"Promise me one thing." Sophia rests her hand on my knee.

"Anything."

"Don't let me go." Sophia's eyes soften as she holds my gaze, but there's a hidden fright behind them lurking in the darkness.

I press my lips to her forehead, gauging the meaning behind her words. Somehow, I think she's referring to more than just tonight. What is she so afraid of?

I pull my lips away, catching her eyes once more. "Not a chance. Besides," I smirk, "according to tomorrow's headlines, ``there's a wedding in our future.''"

I glance at Frank, noticing the rise of his brow. I can't believe I said that. I mean, it is my intention eventually, but not now. I don't want to run her off by moving too fast.

Sophia is quiet for a moment. "Was that a proposal?" She asks playfully.

"Oh sweet, Melody. When I propose to you, there will be no need to ask." I lift her chin with my finger, bringing her lips within a hair's breadth of mine. "But know this. It's destined."

Sophia moves forward, and our lips meet in a simple kiss before she pulls away.

Frank pulls up in front of Melodies a few minutes later, and Sophia and I exit the car and go inside. It's Sunday, so the restaurant is crowded tonight, but the owner always makes room for our band when we call ahead. After our label discovered us here, the owner vowed to always have room for DOL.

We are seated in a corner booth facing each other. A waitress stops next to our table with two menus tucked into her arm and a pen and pad peeking out of the pocket of her waist apron. Her eyes immediately find mine. She gives one menu to Sophia and the other to me. There's a huge smile on her face, and a noticeable blush stains her cheeks. She looks to be around our age and an obvious fan.

"What can I get you to drink, Mr. Daye?" The waitress asks.

I glance at her name tag. "Emily, I'll have a vodka dry with lime and a glass of water." I look at Sophia, who is curiously eyeing Emily.

Emily turns to Sophia. "And you miss?" She asks, uninterested.

"I'll have the same on the rocks," Sophia answered.

My eyebrows rise questioningly, and Sophia tilts her head daringly to one side. I've never seen her drink anything but wine. So, this should be interesting.

Emily scribbles on her notepad, then clicks her pen closed. Her smile returns when she looks at me. "I'll be back to take your order," she says.

Sophia stares at me once Emily is gone. "So that's what I have to look forward to, huh?"

I won't lie to her. Emily is subtle compared to some of our other fans, and that's probably accounted for by her not wanting to lose her job.

"Oh, it gets worse, but you have nothing to worry about, Soph. I'm all yours." I wink, holding my hand out for hers on the table, and she places her hand in mine.

Emily returns with our drinks. Her eyes roll when she notices our joined hands. She sets the glasses in front of us and takes our order.

Sophia and I were still holding hands when Emily returned with our food.

"Let me know if there's *anything* else you need, Mr. Daye," Emily stresses.

Sophia grins, and I rub my thumb soothingly over the back of her hand, reassuring her that I'm here with her. I would be a fool to risk losing her for a fling. That's not what I want anymore.

I keep my eyes on Sophia, and she watches me closely. "Thanks, Emily. I have everything I need right here, but I'll let you know when we're ready for the bill."

Sophia looks up, satisfied. "Thanks, Emily," she says, mirroring my words.

Emily's smile wanes, and she clears her throat. "Well, enjoy." She hurries off with lost hope following behind her.

Sophia and I eat our meals and finish our drinks in peace without interruption from Emily. I fork the last bite of chicken and pasta on my plate.

"Uhm. Can I taste that?" Sophia asks before I can eat it. Buzz from the vodka is present in her glossed eyes. I hadn't expected her to drink it all, but she surprised me.

I've read about the last bite theory before. I smirk, realizing what Sophia's doing. She's testing me.

I lift the fork, bringing it to Sophia's lips. "Open wide, Soph."

Her stunned expression is so much better than the last drop. She blinks several times before her mouth closes over my fork.

I set the fork down, then reached across the table to dust the corner of Sophia's mouth with a napkin.

"One day, Soph, it will all make sense. You'll trust your belief." I brush my thumb over her cheek. I don't blame her. After glimpsing my life firsthand through Emily, it would be hard for anyone to keep the doubt at bay. "I would give my last every time if it means I get to keep you."

Sophia gleams at me, a sexy smile appearing on her face. She scoots down a fraction in the booth, and her toes crawl up my thigh to wade across the growing bulge in my shorts.

I clench my teeth, reaching down to grab her feet.

Sophia pulls in a sharp breath. "I think it's time you take me home."

She doesn't have to tell me twice. "I'll get the check."

Fourteen

Sophia

The world seems so different.

I don't feel the same.

I woke up to the first day of my abnormal life this morning. News of my and Owen's excursion last night is everywhere. Paparazzi are camped outside my gate at home. Ellis is still with Dalton because we got in so late last night, and thankfully so. Owen left this morning so that I could get ready for work. Otherwise, I might not have made it.

Last night was the essence of what dreams are made of. It would have been perfect had I not drank the vodka that left me with a hangover.

I drank a cup of coffee before I left home and took two ibuprofens. My second cup of coffee is secured in my palm as I step inside the main office. It feels like everyone is watching me as I walk through, and they are surely whispering behind my back.

My assistant, Maggie, meets me at my office door. "Let me help you with that." She takes the keys from my hand

and opens the door. We walk inside, and she closes the door behind us.

I set my things in their respective places and plop down in my chair with an audible grunt.

"Long night?" Maggie raised an eyebrow.

"Eventful." I sit up straight, sipping coffee from my cup.

"I'd say so," Maggie agrees. "Everyone's talking," she says, throwing her thumb over her shoulder.

"Everyone needs to mind their own business," I snap, staring at Maggie, and she flinches. "I'm sorry, Maggie. I just. It's a lot to take in all at once."

I thought I was prepared. It isn't my first time being flashed by cameras. I experienced it briefly after my father died, but this time is different. Bigger. This time it's all about me, and though it's not nearly as scandalous, it still carries weight.

"It's quite alright." Maggie sits in one of the leather chairs in front of my desk with her notepad on her lap as she's done since she began working here. "I get it. Well, I don't get it, but I do. You're entitled to your frustration."

"But I don't have the right to take it out on you or anyone else here. I brought this on myself."

"May I ask you a personal question?" Maggie taps her pen continuously on her notepad. My eyes flick to the distraction and back up, and she stops.

"You can ask," I shrug. "But depending on the nature, you may not get an answer."

"Fair enough." Maggie clears her throat. "Are you truly happy?"

I block out everything else for a moment and think of Owen and how I feel when we're together. I smile giddily, feeling my cheeks heat for the first time since we parted this morning.

"Yes."

Dangerously so.

"Well, screw the chaos because none of it matters," Maggie says.

"Thanks, Maggie." I release a long breath. "Now, what's on the agenda for today?"

Maggie looks down at her notepad and begins firing off my appointments for the day. "And you had one cancellation for three, but it's been filled. So, that should keep your mind off of things," she finishes.

Maggie leaves, and my clients arrive like clockwork every two hours with a break in between for lunch. At two fifty-five, I look up when Maggie knocks on my door.

"Your three o'clock is here," She announces.

"Send him in." I stand behind the desk, waiting as I always do to greet my clients.

Moments later, Maggie appears with a young man. "Right this way, Mr. Weatherby," she says, escorting the man inside and offering him a seat, but he holds his hand out for me to shake before he does.

My heart nearly stops, and air lodges in my throat. The tips of my fingers press harshly onto the desk.

Kenneth.

I'm in a silent panicked state of shock. I glance at Maggie for help, but she can't because she doesn't know who he truly is.

Maggie squints her eyes at me. "Miss Conley, are you okay?"

I close my eyes for a moment, trying to figure out how to handle this situation. Kenneth will likely cause a scene if I run out, and I've been in enough headlines for one day.

You're a professional.

You can do this.

I open my eyes, blowing out a calming breath. Then, I shake Kenneth's hand.

"I'm fine, Maggie. You may leave us. Thank you."

Maggie turns to leave, and I jerk my hand away as soon as she does. Kenneth sits in front of me with a sly smirk on his face. I'm at a loss for words.

"It's good to see you, Jo." Kenneth's words slither across my skin like an inflamed rash, spreading out of control.

Kenneth has aged well—same everything, just a little older, and his dark hair is trimmed to perfection. He has always been a handsome guy, but his looks are deceiving.

"What are you doing here?" I seethe, trying not to yell.

Kenneth chuckles maniacally. "You're not happy to see me?" He asks.

"Why would I be? Did you forget what you put me through?"

Kenneth ignores me. "I figured it must be a sign when I woke up to your name sounding on the news. I thought you wanted to be found. So. Here. I. Am. Jo."

Repulsion swirls in my stomach. Not even a suit and tie can hide Kenneth's true colors.

"And I thought you would've gotten a clue by now. I left you years ago. So, why on earth would you think that I wanted this?" I motion my hands between us.

"You needed time to cool off. I get it." Kenneth leans forward, and I step back.

I can't bring myself to sit in front of him like this is normal, as if any of this is okay.

"But now that you have," Kenneth continues, "you can come home, Jo."

Jo.

I hate that I used to love Kenneth, calling me by my shortened middle name. I hate that it used to give me comforting chills. Now it just gives me the creeps.

"Don't call me that," I whisper-shout. "This is my home, and *you* are delusional."

"Am I?" Kenneth stands, walking around my desk to stand next to me. He stares out of my window while I stare at my door, wondering if I should run.

You are stronger than your fiercest enemy.

My mom's words ring inside my head, and I plant my feet, crossing my arms over my belly.

"Yes. You are," I answer.

"Hmm." Kenneth stuffs his hands into his pockets, turning his head in my direction over his shoulder. "What I find interesting is the mention of your son and the fact that he's almost five." Kenneth taunts.

My breathing picks up. Then my heart skips a few beats. *Ellis. Oh, God, Ellis.*

"Call me crazy, but that could only mean one of two things. And I would hate to think that you were cheating on me, Jo. That wouldn't be good for either of us."

I freeze at the feel of Kenneth's finger sliding down my arm.

"It would only take one phone call to make things right," he threatens.

I've been on the receiving end of Kenneth's threats plenty before to know that he always delivers. The truth is the only way out of this, and I knew this would happen. I just thought I'd have a few days to figure it out.

I realize that I don't know this version of Kenneth. He has the same mannerisms, but I don't know how much worse he's gotten—how much more damage he can cause.

"He's yours. He's your son." I blink, waiting for Kenneth's response, a harsh come back, or another threat, but only silence fills the air. The hush is more terrifying than anything. Kenneth doesn't hold his tongue for anyone.

I watch from the corner of my eyes as Kenneth crosses his arms over his chest, staring out the window. I used to be relieved when Kenneth thought before reacting, which didn't happen often. His thinking now is scary.

Kenneth grew up in a respectable family with money and influence. Both things could take Ellis away from me. That's why I never told him about Ellis.

I turn my head in Kenneth's direction and his mouth parts. He releases a long breath. "I have a son," he says, sincerely. He sounds happy, relieved. "What's his name?"

"Ellis."

"Tell me about him," Kenneth says, still looking forward.

I stare at him, confused by his calm demeanor. "You're not upset?"

Kenneth looks at me, smiling, but I see trouble in his gaze. It took me a long time to decipher, pairing his words with his looks and the meaning behind them, but I know now. It's not just happiness or him wanting to know what

Ellis is like. Kenneth wants control, and I've just given him the most valuable bargaining chip he's ever had.

"Why would I be upset?" Kenneth turns in my direction, twisting me toward him and covering the sides of my arms with his hands. "You've given me a family. Yeah, I've missed out on a lot, but you can make it up to me. Starting now. It will be great. You'll see."

I shake my head. "No, Kenneth. I can't. I'm with someone else." I try to pull away from him, but he grips my arms tighter, sending sharp pains through them. He jerks my body forward into his chest, and a gush of air leaves me. Fire and hatred flicker in his eyes, reminding me of the man that I last saw.

"There is no one else. Get rid of the guy, or I will." Kenneth's words are like daggers piercing my heart. His grip lessens, but his hands remain on my arms. The man I knew, the one I just witnessed, slips back into his dark cave, and Kenneth smirks.

A knock sounds at the door, and both of us turn our heads in that direction. Kenneth drops his hands, releasing me from his chest, and I wave Maggie inside. She stops inside the door frame, peeping her head in.

"I'm sorry for interrupting." Maggie's eyes swivel between us. "Just checking to see if you needed anything," she says with worry on her face.

I force a smile, never more grateful for her company. Who knows what Kenneth would have done next if Maggie hadn't noticed? "Mr. Weatherby was just leaving. Would you mind showing him out?" I mentally roll my eyes at the last name that doesn't belong to him.

"Not at all." Maggie widens the door further, waiting for Kenneth.

Kenneth looks at me with the sweetest smile of deception. "So, I'll see you this weekend. I trust you'll have everything sorted by then." He leans forward, placing a kiss on my left cheek and whispering in my ear. "You're mine, Jo."

I stand as still as a steel rod, holding in every emotion because all I can think of is ramming my knee into his nutsack. I have to be smart about this.

Kenneth pulls away and walks toward the door, and I can do nothing but watch as everything that I've built with Owen these past few months follows behind him.

Maggie gives me a sympathetic glance and closes the door behind them. I turn my back to the door, staring out the window. The tears that I'd been holding inside began to fall with my jagged breaths.

Kenneth left me with two choices that are one and the same. Either I lose Owen, or I *lose* Owen. I'm not okay with either of those options. Owen is a part of me now, and I can't imagine a life without him in it. But I can't stand the idea of something happening to him because of me. I have to find a way to let him go. Protecting him and Ellis is more valuable than a broken heart.

Fifteen

Owen

I squeeze Sophia's hand over the armrest on the way to Mom's house. She's been quiet since I picked her up. It's not like her, but drinking vodka wasn't like her either. Maybe she's still feeling the effects.

"Are you feeling up to this tonight, Soph?"

Sophia remains quiet, her eyes focused on something in front of her.

"Soph," I tried again.

"Hmm?" She jerks to life.

"Are you having second thoughts? We could do this another time. Mom will understand."

"No," Sophia says quickly. "Now is perfect. I don't want to waste any more time."

Sophia was fine when I left her this morning. I sense that she's not saying something, but I don't push. Maybe it has to do with the talk she promised me about Ellis' father. Or maybe she's just tired from a long day at work.

"We'll keep the visit short," I suggest. "No dinner, only a meet and greet."

"Owen." Sophia stops me. "You don't have to cut anything short on my account. I've been looking forward to meeting your mom since you came home. We are not bailing." She grins, but it's not full.

"Okay. But if you change your mind."

"I won't."

A few minutes later, we're at Mom's door. I knock then use my key to enter. "We're here," I announce.

Dad is in the living room sitting in the double recliner, and Mom enters moments later with a drink tray in her hands, holding one bottle of beer and a glass of iced lemonade.

"You made it," Mom says with a blank expression. She places the tray on the end table next to dad and turns to face us.

"Mom, Dad, this is Sophia," I responded.

Mom gives Sophia a once-over, managing a condensed smile. "Well, don't just stand there. Offer the young lady a seat." She motions to the sofa to dad's right.

Sophia and I sit, and Mom sits next to dad.

Mom and Dad are not touchy-feely kinds of parents. So, I hope Sophia doesn't take offense.

"Sophia, Owen tells me you're an Estate Planner," Mom says, breaking the silence and getting straight down to business.

"Yes, Ma'am." Sophia straightens next to me, joining her hands on her lap.

"Please, call me Sara. And this handsome log here is Andrew," Mom says, nodding at dad.

"Yes, Ma…. Sara and Andrew," Sophia smiles.

Dad looks at Sophia, his forehead furrowed. "I didn't say you could call me Andrew," He spouts in his lawyer tone.

Sophia winces, her fingers squeezing together. "Uhm, my apologies, Sir. I…."

Dad's laughter fills the air, cutting Sophia's apology short. "Don't apologize," he says. "Andrew is fine. I was only kidding you."

Sophia lets out a timid grin, but her hands are still locked tight. I put my hand over hers, coaxing them apart and entwining my fingers with hers. She glances at me and goes back to my parents.

Dad's not one to joke with everyone he meets. Being a lawyer has hardened him, made him hyper-aware of things that the ordinary person might not notice, and skeptical of everyone breathing. He must sense something in Sophia that he likes since she managed to coax a laugh out of him.

"As I was saying." Mom playfully swats dad's arm with her hand. "Sophia, do you enjoy what you do?"

"I do. It's kind of morbid but also rewarding helping others plan for the future," Sophia answers, and her fingers relax in mine. She always seems at peace when she talks about her job. Her love for it shines in her eyes.

Mom nods, impressed. "And you have a son."

"Yes. Ellis will be five soon," Sophia says, her smile slipping for a moment and returning.

"And how does he feel about this," Mom asks, motioning to Sophia and me.

"Ellis adores Owen. He's happy. He's never had a…." Sophia pauses, reluctant to finish her sentence.

"A what?" Mom raised a brow, her gaze flitting to me for a moment.

I shook my head, silently pleading with her not to pursue this line of questioning. Sophia was already on edge about something else before we arrived. She doesn't need the added stress.

Sophia chews the inside of her cheek.

"Sara," Dad chimes in. "Give Sophia a break. She didn't come here to be drilled. We just met," he says pointedly.

"You're right," Mom says to dad. "Forgive me, Sophia. Owen is my son. My only son, so it's only natural that I'd want to protect him. Something I'm sure you understand."

"I understand," Sophia says. "But with all due respect, your son is a grown man who is more than capable of taking care of himself. And you don't have to protect him from me. I promise to always act in his best interest."

Sophia looks over at me and, fuck; I want to kiss her brains out and make love to her at this very moment. Her eyes leave mine, returning to my parents once more. I keep my eyes on her for a few seconds before doing the same.

Mom looks stunned but pleased.

"I like her, Sara. Don't you?" Dad smirks, a proud, approving look on his face.

The corners of Mom's mouth quirked up. "I do. Brains *and* brass," Mom admires. "I was a little worried at first, but now I'm thinking she'll fit right in."

I lean over and whisper in Sophia's ear, "So fucking cute," and she clears her throat.

"Young love," Dad says, eyeing us closely. "Reminds me of us when we were younger, Sara. To be that age again," Dad sighs, his eyes looking off into the distance. "Things were much easier then. A lot less worry." He strokes his chin between his fingers, then his eyes land on me. "Then, this one came along, and it seemed all we did was worry. It was never a dull moment with him, but I wouldn't change one thing. Not one." Dad smiles, and Mom reaches over and grabs his hand.

He and mom have the same look on their faces—the one that I could never quite decipher. They're acting weird again. Mom notices me watching her, and she lets go of Dad's hand.

"Where are my manners?" She looks at Sophia. "Would you like something to eat or drink, Sophia?"

"Now that you mention it, that lemonade looks tasty," Sophia nods to the drink tray next to Dad.

Mom stands. "In that case, come with me. Owen, you don't mind if I steal her away for a bit, right?"

"Just promise me there will be no childhood stories, please," I beg.

"What would be the fun in that," Mom teases.

I look at Sophia, hoping she understands the question in my gaze. She smiles back at me, giving my hand a soft squeeze before releasing it.

"She'll be fine, Owen. We're only going into the next room," Mom says pointedly.

"Catch up with your dad, Owen. I'm fine." Sophia stands and follows Mom out of the room.

My eyes find Dad's burning a hole through me after they're gone. "You have concerns," I state the obvious. "So, let me have it."

I know Dad well enough to know when he's not totally on board with something. What I don't know is why? I thought seeing her would erase some of their doubt. I assumed earlier that he was fine with our relationship, but now I'm not so sure. My parents are confusing, always have been. I hope Sophia is okay with Mom in the kitchen.

"Sophia is a nice girl," Dad says.

"But…" I press my back against the sofa, resting one hand on my knee.

Dad shrugs. "I'm concerned for the child and what it would do to him if things didn't work out between you two."

"Sophia and I are solid, Dad. It *will* work out."

Dad's skepticism lingers in the air between us. "I'm also worried about you. I've never seen you wrapped up in anything but your music."

"Is that the worst thing in the world?" My irritation spikes.

"Let me ask you this." Dad sits up straight, shooting me an intimidating stare. "Would you give up your music for her, for her son? Because if your answer is no, then you're not ready to be in this kind of relationship. You're dating someone's mother. Someone whose first priority is her child. Someone who would walk away in a heartbeat if she felt like your career was more important than her and her son."

"Yes," I blurted out without a second thought, surprising myself. The idea of music disappearing from my life is painful. I would miss it, but it was never meant to last an entire lifetime. Sophia and Ellis are my future. "What's this about, Dad? Is this truly about Sophia and me, or is it about you and Mom? I see the way you look at me, the way you've always looked at me as if I'm a huge disappointment." I straighten my back, matching Dad's posture, unable to hold back my feelings any longer. "I'm sorry I wasn't the son you've always wanted. I'm sorry that I wasn't worth getting to know. But if you had taken the time, if you hadn't kept me at arm's length, you would know that nothing or no one is going to deter me from Sophia."

"Son." Sympathy crosses Dad's face, or maybe it's regret. He's hard to figure out. "I had no idea you felt that way. I may not have delivered my feelings and intentions in the best way, but you were always my top priority next to your mother. I would do anything for my family. *Anything*," he says sternly.

I know Dad's not lying. I know that he raised me the best way he saw fit. I just don't understand why he chose that route—why he chose to love me from a distance.

"My actions were selfish and had nothing to do with the man you've become. You are exactly who you were meant to be, and I couldn't be prouder. I love you, Son. No matter what. Remember that."

Is he proud of me?

Dad has never been more open with me than he is now. I wasn't prepared for it, and a series of confusing emotions overtook me at once. I clear my throat, blinking back the tears that threaten to fall.

It's hard to believe this is the same man who only spoke words of importance during my childhood. The same man who tried to cast doubt in my mind about my career choice. The same man that never saw me perform.

This man, my father, is proud of me.

I didn't know how much I needed to hear those words until this moment. The boy in me that so desperately craved his father's approval cries with joy. But he weeps for the man in me, for lost time that he and his father will never get back again. Knowing how my father feels doesn't make up for anything, but it will help me heal and move forward.

A hug feels warranted but out of place. It's not usual behavior. Instead, I say, "Thanks, Dad," because it's the only thing that makes sense for us.

We fall into a heavy silence, and a few minutes later, Mom and Sophia reappear with two glasses of lemonade. Sophia looks okay, but I can't be certain if she faced Mom's inquisition while she was away or not. If their talk was anything like mine and Dad's, I could only imagine what she was thinking.

Sophia and I stayed for another half hour, opting out of dinner. We picked Ellis up from Dalton's before I took them home, and he went straight to bed once inside.

Sixteen

Sophia

I stare at Owen expectantly once I'm sure Ellis is settled in for the night. "Take a shower with me," I suggested. All I want to do is wash the evening away and soak up the time we have left. I have less than a week to rip us to shreds. Four days to accept that Owen won't be mine anymore.

Kenneth isn't the only one against my and Owen's relationship. Owen's parents, though apologetic, made themselves very clear. I'm not what they want for their son. And who could blame them? I'm not exactly picture-perfect.

"I'm on board with that," Owen smirks, sweeping his fingers through his hair and stalking toward me from the bedroom door.

Every step he takes toward the bed streams in slow motion inside my head. Every step is painfully breathtaking, matching the beats of my bruised heart. His taut skin accentuates the toned muscles in his arms as he lifts his shirt over his head and throws it to the floor.

Owen stops in front of me, and I flatten my palm over his heart, feeling it pound, reaching out to me. I press my lips to the center of his chest as his lips settle on my forehead and his hands on my hips. I pull in a slow breath as his hands slide up my side, taking my shirt with them. I close my eyes, releasing that same breath as his thumbs brush over my breast. He removes my shirt, then reaches around and unclasps my bra. His fingers trace my backbones, catching my straps, pulling them over my shoulders, and dropping my bra to the floor.

I gaze deep into his eyes, blocking out everything else around us. "Kiss me."

Owen's eyes search mine, scorching my soul, branding it, and ruining me for all others. His palms circle my face, and he obliges, kissing me with a passion I've never felt before. Our tongues dance to our silent melody. We lose the rest of our clothes somewhere between the beats, and Owen lifts me, carrying me into the shower. He turns the water on while peppering kisses at the base of my neck. The cool spray drains over my head, soothing my heated skin.

Owen turns us, and my back hits the opposite wall with a soft thud. "Shower. Check. Kiss. Check." He covers my breast with his mouth, sucking, then releasing it. "I could kiss you all night, Soph. But I get the feeling that's not all you want." He looks at me expectantly, then pulls my other breast into his mouth, repeating the action. My chest heaves as his eyes find mine again. "I won't do it unless you tell me."

I know what he's saying, what we're both thinking. We're exposed, open, raw. I'm on the pill. We've both been tested, and right now, that's all that matters. Whatever happens, happens. There are no mistakes.

I want to be reckless.

I want to feel him without anything between us for the first and last time.

"Fuck me like you love me."

Owen's eyes darken. His hands hold firm to my thighs. "Hold on," he rasps.

I clasp my arms around his neck as he positions himself and eases inside of me. A soft moan escapes my mouth. Owen buries himself to the hilt, grunting into my neck.

Ellis is my one percent blessing. It's the first time that I've been skin to skin with anyone, and it's ten times better than I imagined.

Owen's palm slaps the wall beside my head, and his other hand grips my ass. "Fuck." His breath washes over my skin like the sweetest sin. Every letter, a different meaning. Every stroke, a sacred promise. Like a song unsung, made especially for me.

Forever.

Unconditional.

Complete.

Kalon.

My back slides easily against the porcelain tile as I match the motion of his hips. He pulls my nipple into his mouth, teasing it between his teeth, eliciting a moan from me. His lips travel up to my neck.

"Perfect," Owen breathes. "Devine." His tongue snaked out to taste me. "Mine," he says, clamping his mouth over my collar bone and sucking.

"Yours," I concur. I will always be Owen's, even though we can't be together. The thought excites me and haunts me, my thighs clenching and releasing around him conflicted.

Owen looks into my eyes. I keep one arm around his neck, bringing the other to the side of his face. Our lips crash together in a heated kiss as we continue our movements. He slams into me again and again. My entire body aches with pleasure, my center contracting as my love spills over him. My body pulses, and I whimper, "Aah." My eyes close, releasing a few tears, and my mouth hangs open, breath wisping into his mouth.

It's too much, yet, not nearly enough.

Owen slows his movement to a crawl. "Soph, tell me to stop," he pleads, dropping his head to the crook of my neck. I can feel him thicken further inside me. Feel the throbbing of his shaft. "I don't. I can't," he mumbles around the slow grooves of motion, the heat from his lips piercing my skin.

"I want," is all I can manage to say, but *more* rings loudly inside my mind.

I want everything that Owen has to give before this night is over.

Everything.

"Soph," Owen says again, still kissing my neck.

I respond by sliding my back up the wall and back down, covering him.

Owen reciprocates. Both of his hands grip my ass now as he begins to move faster, more urgently, pounding into me, until his body jerks then stalls inside of me with a grunt.

Owen steps away from the wall an inch, and I drop my legs, my body sliding against his until my feet reach the floor.

We're quiet. Shameless. Sated.

I can't think of anything that would make this moment better.

But in random Owen fashion, he surprises me once again by turning us around toward the gentle spray of the water. He grabs a sponge, coating it with body wash, and cleanses every inch of me before taking care of himself.

He takes me to bed when we're done, and I'm in complete awe. I refuse to think about anything but us tonight. The way his body curves around my backside. The weight of his arms around me. His warm breath at the back of my head. The sincerity in his voice as he whispers, *"I love you, Soph,"* right before his breathing evens out.

I close my eyes to his words as they trickle into my heart, and a lone tear slips out.

A tear of joy masking the pain.

• • • • • ♩ ♪ ♩ • • • • •

My eyes strain open against the morning sun. Memories of last night come rushing back, putting a smile on my face. A pair of muscled thighs block my vision next to the bed. I blink, slowly tilting my head up, letting my eyes roam free until they reach Owen's welcoming gaze.

Thank God for shorts because I'd be all over him had they not been there.

"I made coffee," Owen smirks, sitting the covered mug next to the bed.

It has got to be the worst form of karma. It has to be. Owen is too good to be true, except he is very true, and I can't keep him.

What's the point of having something nice and shiny if I have to give it back? It's like having a fancy rental car that comes with all the bells and whistles—better than anything that I've ever had before. But like all things, there's a catch. It's taunting, *"You can keep me, but I come at a cost that you don't want to pay."*

"Good morning." I smiled at him. "Thanks." I nod to the coffee.

In a covered mug.

My brows furrow. I lift my cell phone to check the time and shoot straight up in bed.

"Whoa," Owen says, placing a hand on my shoulder. "Relax."

"Relax? Relax? I have a client at eight." I fling the covers off of me frantically. "What happened to my alarm?" I look at the phone again, confused.

"I turned it off when you didn't wake up." Owen shrugs. "I figured you needed the extra rest." He grabs my hand and sits next to me on the bed. "Don't worry about Ellis today. I don't have anything else to do until practice later. So, he can hang with me. Maybe I'll take him fishing." He smiles, and butterflies fill my belly.

"You fish?"

"No, but I'd learn, for Ellis, if it's something he wanted to do."

Tears threaten to cloud my vision, but I blink them away.

You will not cry.

You will not cry.

But if there was ever a reason to cry, this moment is worthy. Owen always finds a way to cripple my heart, then give it a reason to beat again. I had planned on ending things this morning, but how can I?

"If that's okay with you," Owen continued.

I bring my palm to his cheek and press my lips to his. "Thank you."

Owen chuckles, brushing my hair behind my ear. "For what?"

"For being true to who you are. For being the man I never knew I needed. For lending me your heart."

Owen grabs my hand, bringing it to his chest, resting over his heart. "It's not a loan, Soph. So don't even try giving it back because it's not mine anymore. While I breathe, it's yours. And even after, it remains."

Owen tilts my chin, kissing me, and I lose all sense of reason until he pulls away. "Now, go. Get ready for work."

I want to protest, to say screw work, but I can't because I'm a responsible adult—a fact that I have to remind myself of daily since Owen came along.

Seventeen

Owen

Dinner is on me tonight.

I looked over the message I had just typed out for Sophia and hit send. It's been an interesting couple of days. Sophia has been quieter than not, and I wonder if it has anything to do with my impending trip. We still haven't had that talk yet about Ellis' dad, and I'm starting to believe that she doesn't want me to know about him. What kind of guy could he have been to make her feel the way she does?

I pull the bill of my cap down to my eyebrows. A smile curves my lips as I exit the car. Frank accompanies me into Packard's Grocery for supplies. Packard's is a mom-and-pop grocery store that's been here since I can remember, but my parents never shopped here.

Frank didn't leave me with much choice today. When I first mentioned shopping, he wasn't too keen on the idea, countering that I could just order what I needed or have him pick it up, but I insisted. I want to do something nice for Sophia and Ellis before I leave on Sunday. I want every aspect of tonight to be a labor of love, and it's less likely someone will notice or make contact with me here. So, I compromised.

    I don't enjoy that I have to leave soon. I understand how the guys feel now, being away from their families. Sophia and I had been apart for two weeks before, and that was hard. A month is a long time, and I imagine it will be harder, but I can't avoid it unless I quit. So, I plan to cherish every moment she allows for the next two days.

    The old-fashioned bell rings above the door when I open it to enter the store. The space is cozy, smaller than everything that I'm used to. It reminds me of a convenience store with a few more low-rise aisles, and they sell meat and fruit along with the usual staples. A young boy is standing behind the cash register, and his head swivels in our direction as we enter. He stares for a moment, then nods. I'm not sure if he recognizes me or if he's watching because I look suspicious. I'm the first to look away.

    It's the beginning of the workday, so not many people are inside. Those that are shopping are mostly older men and women, whom I imagine come at this time to avoid the younger crowd. Everyone is focused on what they're doing, and I'm grateful.

    I grab a small cart and walk the aisles, picking out what I need along the way. Then, I select a variety of meat and cheese from the back wall and their nicest bottle of red wine. I throw in a bag of gummies and a bag of chips for Ellis.

A woman steps from the back when I reach the front of the store. She glances at me and smiles, stopping next to the boy at the register, whose face resembles hers. She must be the owner. Her name badge reads Bonnie, and his, Donald.

Bonnie hands Donald a piece of paper, and he reads it, stuffing it into his pocket. Then, she looks at me. She tilts her head, squinting her eyes, and her smile falters for a moment. Her mouth parts and closes. Then it opens again.

"You're Owen. Owen Daye," Bonnie says with a calm excitement that I'm not accustomed to.

It's hard to tell which way this conversation is headed. So, I act as normal as she appears.

"That's me." I smile back at her, thankful that she didn't scream my name.

"Mom talks about your band all the time," Donald says, finally showing an ounce of interest.

Bonnie smacks the side of his arm. "Shush, child."

"Hey. It's true." Donald feigns offense.

"Well, I am a fan," Bonnie says. "But don't worry. I won't out you. You're here." She motions to the space around us. "So, I gather you want to remain incognito."

I empty my items onto the countertop. "I think that would be best."

"Not a problem," Bonnie says as Donald begins ringing things up. "Did you find everything you needed?" She looks down at my selection. "Perhaps a rose for the young lady?" She questions.

Frank snickers behind me.

I should be alarmed by Bonnie's suggestion, but I'm not. She seems like a nice sane lady, and her tip isn't half bad. It's not bad at all. "Sure. What gave me away?"

"No offense, but you don't strike me as a red wine type of guy." Bonnie chuckles.

"That obvious, huh?"

"No. Mom read it in some magazine. That your drink of choice was vodka," Donald snitches, and I laugh quietly.

"That's enough, Donald." Bonnie shoots him an evil eye, then looks back at me. "I'm not a stalker. I promise. Not the bad kind." She clears her throat. "Anyway, I'm sure we have taken enough of your time." She picks the most perfect rose out of the batch and hands it to me. "On the house."

"You don't have to…."

"Please. It's the least I can do."

I pay for the rest of my groceries and pull one of the cards that Justin insists we carry around out of my wallet. It's folded in two, but it will do.

I scribble an I.O.U. on the back with my autograph and their names. "If you ever want to see us in action live, just show up and bring this card with you. They'll take care of you."

"Thanks," Bonnie beams.

I'm grateful that we managed to get into and out of the store without issues. I look back at the store as Frank pulls away and spot Bonnie standing in front of the glass window, thinking, *maybe I'll see her again at one of our performances.*

• • • • • ♩ ♪ • • • • •

I stopped by Sophia's office earlier to confiscate her key and let her know that I would pick Ellis up from Dalton's and bring him with me to get dinner ready before she came home. Ellis was excited and happy to be involved.

"She's home! She's home!" Ellis shouts, hearing Sophia's car pull into the garage.

I love Ellis' enthusiasm. I'll miss him while I'm away the next month. I'm not his father, but he and I are like best buds, in a father-son kind of way.

We meet Sophia at the door, welcoming her home. She sniffs the air, trying to figure out what we made for dinner.

"That's cheating, Mom," Ellis chastises.

"Is not," She teases, bending to tickle his belly, sending him into a fit of laughter.

"No fair," Ellis giggles, escaping Sophia's hold. He runs, stopping next to the table.

I pull Sophia back against me, kissing the side of her neck. "I missed you."

"Ewe, gross!" Ellis looks away, gaining a chuckle from Sophia and me.

"Go get settled and hurry back," I tell Sophia.

She glances over her shoulder. "Well, since you asked nicely," she grins, stepping away from me.

"Hurry," I say again, lightly smacking her ass.

Sophia returns moments later, and Ellis ushers her to the table where she sits, waiting for our creation. Her eyes widened when I set dinner in front of her.

"You made—pizza?" Sophia glances at Ellis, then at me.

"Mhm," Ellis nods proudly. "And pasta."

She looks surprised and a little disappointed behind her smile.

"It's not just any pizza," I wiggle my eyebrows. "This one's special." I bend down next to her ear, whispering, "The kind that makes you want to climb poles and do naughty things."

Sophia sucks in a breath, and I laugh, moving to sit across from her at the table. She glances at Ellis and back at me, raising a brow.

"Totally ineffective on kids," I answered her unspoken question.

"Owen said we had to wait on you, and you're here. So, can we eat now?" Ellis looks expectantly at Sophia.

"Sure, Bud." Sophia smiles at Ellis. Then, her eyes meet mine. *"Thank you,"* she mouths.

I wink, smiling back at her. "Let's eat."

Minutes tick by, and we devour every drop of pizza before us. Then, we moved to the living room and watched a movie with Ellis. Sophia and I retire to the bedroom once Ellis is asleep in his bed.

I've spent more nights at her place than mine in the last week at her request. It's like she's making up for lost time or trying to compensate for our impending time apart. Either way, I don't mind being here.

Sophia haphazardly moves her fingers over the back of my hand, resting on her belly as we lie in bed. "Do you ever feel like the closer you get to the things you want, they get further and further out of reach?"

"It's funny that you ask that." I rub my thumb over the soft skin of her belly. My chest is pressed against her back. Heat runs warm through her body to mine, soothing us both.

"How so?" She glances over her shoulder.

She just described what I felt. Being here this week made me feel much closer to her, but I can't help but notice that she's pulling away. Obviously, she feels the same. Otherwise, she wouldn't have brought it up. But I don't get why.

"Well, you seem kind of distant lately. Is it because I'm going away?"

"No. I knew what I signed up for. It's not that," Sophia sighs.

"What is it then?"

Sophia is quiet for a long moment before she turns to face me. My arms remain draped over her waist, and her palm flattens on my chest.

"I think it's time I tell you about Ellis' father."

I've waited weeks for this conversation, and now, I don't know if I'm ready to hear what she has to say. The prolonged suspense put a lot of thoughts in my head that I couldn't shake. "I'm all ears," I joke to lighten the mood.

Sophia doesn't react. Her eyes portray sadness, and her lips form a straight line. "Do you want the long version or the condensed version?"

"Whatever you want me to know. I'm listening."

Sophia nods, clearing her throat. "Kenneth and I met in college at a time when I was still figuring things out. I thought he was the man I'd spend the rest of my life with."

My fingers unconsciously tighten on her side at the thought.

"He was a dream until he wasn't," Sophia continued. "It took years for me to realize that him requiring so much of my time was his way of keeping track of me, controlling me. I thought that his jealousy meant he cared. I brushed off our heated arguments because I believed that every couple fights. And when he hit me for the first time, I was the one who apologized." She pauses, lowering her eyes to my chest.

I opened my mouth and closed it, trying to process what she told me.

"I stayed for months after because I believed him every time he said he would change, he'd do better. But even more complicated than that was his family's reputation. I felt like I didn't have a choice."

I feel the warmth of her tears on my arm under her head. I circle my hand soothingly on her back, attempting to offer some kind of comfort.

"The night I left him was the last straw. I didn't care about the choice I didn't have anymore. All I could think about at that moment was what would happen if I had stayed in that toxic relationship. It didn't matter what choice I made. I was screwed either way," she sniffs, and her hand twitches on my chest.

"My mother picked me up from his place and took me home that night. I considered going back to Kenneth the next morning, but my mom took me to the hospital instead. I could barely move my arm, and a plum-sized bruise had formed on my cheek. Mom insisted that I tell the cops what happened, but I refused, making up the biggest lie I had ever told. But she refused to let me go back." Sophia sniffs again, and her tears continue to soak my arm.

A sad chuckle leaves her, and she continues. "I've never told Dalton this, but our father had a hand in saving my life. It's because of him and my mother that I'm here. If it hadn't been for them...."

Sophia's words trailed off, and I finally understood why she had reacted to me the way she did in the beginning. She'd been hurt in one of the worst ways possible, and I threatened her security.

"I found out that I was pregnant the morning after Kenneth assaulted me, and my whole world changed. Suddenly, *I* had someone to protect, someone to live for, and I wasn't going to let Kenneth take that away from me. So, I left, and I never told him about Ellis." She confesses.

"Soph," I whispered, tilting her chin with my finger and bringing her red-rimmed eyes back to mine. "I'm sorry you had to go through that."

"No. Don't apologize for his actions. You are not him, and I know that now. You helped me to see that." Sophia brings her hand to my cheek. "He tried to take everything from me, made me feel worthless, and you.... You replaced all of that hurt, pain, and anger with love. You are such a man, Owen Daye, and I love you for it." A grateful, sad smile curves her lips.

I pull her flush against me, speaking close to her lips. "I love you more." I hold her gaze, wondering how someone, once broken and so beautiful, could fall for a guy like me.

"I'm going to miss you, Owen." Sophia's sullen tone cracks my heart wide open.

I nuzzle my nose against hers. "I'll be back before you know it. It's only a month, and I'm always a phone call away." I brush my thumb over her lips.

"There's something else you should know," Sophia says, and I wait because what could be worse than what she's already told me? "Kenneth stopped by my office on Monday."

I freeze, thinking that I heard her wrong at first. I search her eyes for an explanation, and confusion clouds my vision. Questions swim inside my head.

Why did he show up now?

What did he want?

What does this mean for Ellis?

And the most blaring one of all….

Why didn't you tell me?

I realize now that he's the reason for her mood this week. Her reason for keeping me close and pushing me away. Every question I can think of seems minute and accusatory. So, I ask the one that's most sincere, most important.

"Are you okay?"

"I'm fine, but I, we…." A tear slipped from the corner of her eyes, trailing over her nose.

"We'll be fine, Soph. I'm not going anywhere. My bark is stronger than his. We'll get through this together. I won't let him hurt Ellis or you again."

Sophia's tears fall freely at my words, and she presses her lips to mine.

I now realize that I wasted my life outside of music. I can't remember half of what it was spent on. But I remember every moment I've had with Sophia and Ellis from the beginning until now. I'm in love with Sophia, and I love Ellis as if he were my flesh and blood, my son. They are my family, and I would never turn my back on them.

Eighteen

Sophia

Owen groans, "Mmm," snuggling close to me at daybreak as we lie in bed. "No regrets." He whispers behind me. His arms cocoon me, and I can't ignore his morning wood firmly pressed at my backside.

"Good morning." I try to be cheerful, but my voice betrays me.

Owen being here is dangerous for him, but I don't have the courage to let him go. I close my eyes, wanting to cry all over again because it has to be done. The more I prolong this, the worse it will be.

"One more day." Owen pulls my hair back, placing one kiss after another on my shoulder.

My heart shatters because I'm not even sure if we have today. "That's the saddest truth you've ever spoken."

Owen chuckles into my neck, unaware of how serious I am. "So, how do you want to spend it?"

Running away with you.

From you.

"I don't know." My thoughts are at war, and I let them rage inside my head. "Our current state is nice, but I doubt it will fly with Ellis here."

"I have an idea." Owen braces himself, leaning over me, and I turn my head in his direction.

"What?" I grin.

"I have to run home to pack. Want to come with me?"

"Not if you plan to get anything done."

Owen's eyes trail down my body and back up to my eyes. "You're probably right." He licks his lips, eyes steaming over me, bringing heat to my skin. Then he kisses me slowly and steadily before pulling away. His eyes focus back on mine. "You've ruined me, Soph." His thumb traces the curve of my mouth.

You've ruined me too.

I want to frown and cry, but I keep the semblance of a smile plastered on my face instead. "You've given me so much to remember in a short amount of time. I'll hold on to that. I'll cling to the memories of you, Owen. Always."

Owen kisses me once more, then gets out of bed. I watch him closely, my mind grasping even the slightest movement he makes and tucking them into my mental closet.

Owen stops next to the bed, grabbing the house keys. "I won't be long." Then he's gone.

I get out of bed and fumble my way through getting washed and dressed, feeling like I need to wake up from a good dream gone wrong.

Ellis woke up shortly after I was done. The sight of him both lifted my spirits and made me nauseous. I left him to finish getting dressed while I took a breather for myself.

I don't know how to explain any of this to him. How do I tell him that his father suddenly showed up, and the man he fashioned as a dad will no longer be around? That the month he had expected turned into forever?

A heavy sigh escapes me as I rest my head on the back of the couch with my eyes closed. I wrap my arms around my belly as sharp pain sprints through. Butterflies mix with tension. Rage wrestles with calm.

A tear trickles down my face, and I whisper, "I can't do it."

"Can't do what, Mom?"

My eyes shot open, and I quickly wiped the tear away, attempting a smile.

"Nothing, Bud."

Ellis tilts his head to one side, staring at me. "Are you crying?"

I swear this kid has the instincts of an elder. *Just like Owen.* I grin despite how I feel.

"I'm just a little tired. That's all," I deflect, holding out my arms to Ellis. "Come Here."

Ellis sits next to me, studying me with his lips pursed as if he doesn't believe my excuse.

"I need to tell you something, Bud." I wrap my arms around him and kiss the side of his head.

I have to do this.

The last thing I want is for Ellis to be surprised by Kenneth's sudden presence.

I release him, taking his hands in mine. Then, I release a long breath through my nose.

"Remember when I said I didn't know where your father was?"

Ellis nods. "Yes."

"Well, I do now. Your father surprised me with a visit a few days ago."

Ellis' brows bunch together as if he's in deep thought, and I give him a moment to process what I've said.

"He doesn't want to see me?" Ellis asked.

I feel like I'm explaining this all wrong. I did what I did to protect Ellis, but my heart hurt for him at this moment. I can't help but think that I cheated him out of knowing his father because it's the truth. I just couldn't risk Kenneth taking Ellis away from me, and now I'm again faced with the same situation.

"He does. He wants to see you, but it's complicated." *So complicated.* "Would you be okay meeting him?"

"I think so." Ellis blinks innocently at me. "Is he going to take me away?"

Yes, if I don't do what he wants me to do.

The thought constantly blares inside my mind. It's so much harder than it should be. Am I not allowed to be happy and free? Why is this happening to me?

"No," I speak too firmly, startling Ellis. "I'll never let that happen. No one will ever take you away from me. No matter what. Understand?"

Ellis nods. "Is he coming today?"

I'm stumped for a moment on how to answer that. Kenneth didn't exactly give a date and time.

"I don't know. He said he wanted to surprise me again."

"Do I call him Dad?"

I give Ellis' hand a gentle squeeze and smile. "I'll leave that up to you to decide, but his name is Kenneth Hawthorne."

"Is he moving in with us?"

"I don't think so, Bud." I'm not sure what Kenneth's plans are, but I will not have him living in the home that my father secured so that I could be rid of him.

"Mom?"

"Yes, Bud."

"Why can't Owen be my dad?"

I suck in a breath, caught in the thick of my drama. Owen is more of a dad to Ellis than Kenneth ever will be, and it's my fault. I shouldn't have let Owen in. If I had kept to myself, Owen, Ellis, and I would be safe from this emotional torment.

I don't want to give Ellis false hope, but I don't want to crush his spirit either.

"I can't answer that, Bud." I press my back to the couch, sighing with my eyes looking past Ellis' shoulder. "Life is messy that way. One day it all makes sense, and the next...." I pause, realizing I'm rambling. I look back at Ellis. "Let's just take it one day at a time, okay. You may not understand everything now, but I promise that one day it will all make sense."

At least, I hope so.

I pull Ellis in for a hug that's more for me than for him. Then, I ruffle his already messy hair and release him.

"Mom," Ellis wines, and I laugh, noticing the signs of him getting older. "I'm hungry," he says, glancing in the direction of the kitchen.

Owen should be back with breakfast soon, but I doubt Ellis wants to wait.

"Come on. Let's see what we've got." We stand, and I follow Ellis into the kitchen. I fix him a bowl of cereal, then leave him to it.

The doorbell rings about twenty minutes later, and I smile on my way to open it, thinking it's someone in the family. They are the only ones with access to my gate.

The air is sucked out of my lungs when my eyes fall on Kenneth standing across the threshold. His conniving smirk is like a knife piercing my skin over and over again. His hands are tucked into his front pockets, and he's gorgeous—the devil in disguise. My blood boils in the worst way possible, but I don't react. I can't because Ellis is in his room.

"What are you? How did you get past the gate?"

"Still not happy to see me," Kenneth says, completely ignoring my question. "I'll give it a little longer. In time, you'll change your mind about me, Jo." He chuckles, and I fume, sure that my cheeks are red.

"You could have warned me that you were on the way."

"I warned you the last time we spoke. Or have you forgotten? Besides, what fun would that be?" He winks, then tilts his head to peer around me. "Aren't you going to invite me in?"

"I'm surprised you even asked."

Kenneth's eyes snap to mine, and he raises a brow. One hand leaves his pocket, and he caresses my chin between his thumb and forefinger. "I've missed your spunk, Jo," he mused before stepping past me, brushing his shoulder to mine. "Where's my son?"

"Kenneth, wait. Please." I close the door, hurrying in front of him. I hate the plea that left my mouth and loathe the pleas that are sure to come after it. But it's necessary, worth it, to keep Ellis safe. "Please," I say again. "He's just a child. Let's take this slow. Have a seat, and I'll go and get him."

I'm on the verge of tears, but I refuse to let Kenneth see me cry.

Kenneth stares at me for a few seconds before turning and walking into the living room. So, I walk in the opposite direction, taking his silence for agreement.

I find Ellis in his room watching cartoons and quickly explain that his father did surprise me. He follows me into the living room staying close by my side. Kenneth turns to face us from his spot by the window. His eyes fall to Ellis, and he falters, opening his mouth and closing it.

I've never seen Kenneth nervous, but at that moment, I do believe that he was. It was an endearing, fleeting emotion that washed over him in a matter of seconds.

"Ellis, here is your father." I gesture in Kenneth's direction.

Ellis glances at me, then back to Kenneth, staring as if to say what's next.

Kenneth walks cautiously toward us, stopping two feet away. "Hey, little man," he says smoothly to Ellis.

"I'm not little," Ellis says respectfully.

I watch Kenneth closely, gauging his reaction. There are moments when I see him so clearly in Ellis—all of the good parts. I just hope the bad parts didn't carry over too.

Kenneth chuckles. "That's just the kind of thing I would've said at your age."

Ellis holds his stance, not cracking a smile. I wonder what's going through his mind? Whether he wants to flee? I had an awkward meeting like this with my father once. So, I get the need to be cautious of a familiar stranger. I wanted to hide when I first met my father. I was happy, sad, and confused. And like Ellis, the words just weren't there when we came face to face.

"Let's have a seat," I suggest, thinking of Ellis and how he might feel with someone he doesn't know looking down on him. It can be a little intimidating.

Kenneth glances at me, nodding, and we sit with him on the sofa next to us. He focuses his attention back on Ellis. "So, if you're not little, that must mean you're starting school soon, right?"

"Yes, I'm going to kindergarten," Ellis answers proudly, smiling, finally showing emotion. He and Kenneth continue their question-and-answer session while I listen from the sidelines.

Ellis seems to be at ease with Kenneth being here, and I'm grateful for that. I find myself relaxing and smiling right along with them. Minutes pass, and for a moment, I forget the bad parts of Kenneth, all of the havoc he's capable of. He always had a way of drawing my mind away from his hurtful actions and drawing me into his charm. And this time, he's done it, to the point where I hadn't heard the front door open.

"Soph?"

My head snaps in Owen's direction, standing in the awning of the living room. There's a white bag in his hand, and the smell of pancakes and bacon fills the room. I stood quickly, struck silent. Kenneth stands a few feet away from me.

"Owen!" Ellis says excitedly, jumping up and running to him.

I want to run too, but instead, I hold Owen's gaze, afraid of what I might see if I look at Kenneth. Owen looks at Kenneth and comes back to me. If he's angry, it's hidden well. There's only shock and confusion on his face. I imagine he feels the same as I did when Kenneth popped up in my office and again outside my front door.

Ellis throws his arm around Owen, drawing a smile from him as he looks down at Ellis.

"Hey, Bud. Want to do me a favor?" Owen asks, and Ellis nods. "Take this into the kitchen for me, and give Mom and me a minute to talk."

Ellis agrees, grabbing the bag from Owen's hand and leaving me between a rock and a hard place.

I finally took a brave look at Kenneth. The expression he greeted me with upon arrival is back in full force, except it's directed at Owen. But he's walking toward me.

Oh, God, I'm going to be sick.

Kenneth stops next to me, placing his hand on the small of my back. "You didn't tell me that company was coming over, Jo."

I step away from Kenneth's touch, attempting to go to Owen.

"Jo," Kenneth says my name like a warning, and I stop, my eyes closing for three long seconds. "Careful. Our son is in the next room."

I pull in a deep breath and let it out, turning to face Kenneth. "You have what you want. Just give me a few minutes with him." I hope my eyes are pleading enough, convincing enough to tame Kenneth, even for a few minutes while I rip my heart out and stomp it into the ground.

Kenneth smirks, glancing over my shoulder at Owen and back to me. "Don't make me wait too long," he says, clipping my chin and releasing it.

I walk over to Owen and grab his hand, pulling him with me outside the front door to keep the conversation away from Ellis.

Nineteen

Owen

Sophia and I stop at the edge of the porch, and I stare straight ahead. I fear that my words won't come out right if I look at her. She grips my hand as if she's afraid I'll let go, and I hold hers just the same.

"Did you invite him here, Soph?"

She wouldn't. Would she? Not after what she told me.

Seeing her and Ellis on the couch with her ex burned. They resembled a real family, perfect, mom, dad, child, happy.

Kenneth being here was enough, but I never would've expected Sophia to look at him the way she had when I walked in. Her smile wasn't forced. It was as genuine as every smile she's ever shown me.

I feel betrayed.

"Owen, it's not what you think. I didn't know he was coming. It's what Kenneth does. I don't even know how he got past the gate," Sophia explains.

I give her an incredulous look. "I suppose he broke into the house too, huh?"

"Well, no. I opened the door, but it was too late by that time. I had to think about Ellis, Owen. I couldn't cause a scene." Sophia's eyes plead for me to understand.

The mention of Ellis calms me, and a rush of air leaves my lungs. I close my eyes and open them, turning to face her. "So, what do you need from me?"

"I just need you to understand," Sophia says, stepping closer to me. "I need you to know that you are the best thing that's ever happened to me. You are incredible, Owen, but all of this, us, was painlessly gotten. And there's a hard lesson to be learned from anything that comes easy. Being with you taught me many things." She places her palm on my cheek. "What love is supposed to be. How to be mindful and selfless."

My brows pull together as I stare into her eyes. "What do you need?" I ask again because her words sound a lot like parting words and not the, *we're in this together* kind.

"I need you to leave."

I shake my head. "You can't mean that. I can't lose you, Soph. And what about Ellis?" I let go of her hand, cupping my hands around her face.

"Ellis is not your son, Owen."

Sophia's eyes cloud over, and she clamps her mouth shut. I can see that this is hurting her just as much as it's hurting me. So why is she doing it?

"Tell me you don't mean it," I try again, but my words seem to go over her head. "I can't be there for you if you won't let me."

"I know, which is why I asked you to leave."

A tear drips from Sophia's eyes, and I kiss it away. Then, I tilt my head to kiss her lips. Sophia grips the shirt covering my chest as she kisses me back. There's nothing rushed about it, but somehow it feels final. I love it, and I hate it, the way it makes me yearn for more of what I'm about to lose.

I can't pull away. So, Sophia does it for me, brushing her tears away with her fingers.

"I'm sorry, Owen. I can't do this. I can't love you because if I do…. I just can't. Please accept that." Sophia tries to step away from me, and I pull her back, searching her eyes for an explanation.

"Did he threaten you, Soph?" I glance at the house and back to her.

Sophia doesn't answer, but her silence speaks volumes. This time, I let go, attempting to go back inside.

Sophia's small hands wrap firmly around my arm, stopping me. "Owen, don't. There was a choice. It was my decision," she tells me. "I have to do this for Ellis."

"And what about you? You deserve to be happy."

"What we shared was good, and you've spent only a sliver of your life with me. Now it's time for you to move on to something better. Something extraordinary." Sophia smiles sadly. "You'll always have my heart, Owen. Always." Her palms rest on my chest as she continues to stare up at me. "But you have to let me go." Then, her eyes close, and I allow her to step out of my arms and turn away from me.

My instincts tell me that this is wrong, that I should do something. But what can I do if Sophia's already made up her mind? She's keeping something from me. I can feel it, but she's right. This isn't about me. It's about Ellis, and if Sophia thinks that she and I being apart is best for him, then who am I to protest?

All I can do is watch her walk away. I won't force something on her that she doesn't want. That wouldn't make me any better than Kenneth.

Sophia pauses with her hand on the doorknob, but she doesn't look back when she says, "I've made a lot of mistakes, Owen. Just know that you were not one of them." Then, she disappears behind the door.

· · · · · ♩♪ ♪ · · · · ·

Sleep evaded me last night, leaving room for sulking and wonder.

There were many things that I wanted to do, many things that I had almost done since I last saw Sophia. But with each thought, Ellis would cross my mind, flushing away those thoughts. I would never do anything to hurt him or his mother. I only wish I could hear her voice one last time. Talk to Ellis one last time. I didn't even get to say goodbye.

The last place I want to be is on a plane, flying away from the only woman I've ever loved. Not knowing if there was a way we could work it out is killing me.

I know what Sophia said. I know I let her walk away, but I couldn't help but try. Though, my texts and calls went unanswered. I've lost her, and in losing her, I've lost a part of myself.

I guess this tour couldn't have come at a better time. The best thing for me is to focus on music to keep myself from drowning in pain. But even that's hard to do now with Sophia blended into the fabric of my life. She's my happy place, the chord in my strings, my unsung melody.

"You okay, Owen?" Dalton eyes me from across the aisle of the plane.

We've been in the air for over an hour now and should reach our destination soon.

Luke is passed out in the reclined seat directly across from me. I kind of wish I was where he is so that Dalton couldn't see my face. I promised him that Sophia and Ellis would be safe with me, and she made me break that promise.

No. Never again.

"I will be." I wonder if Dalton knew what Ellis' dad put Sophia through. "Can I ask you a question?"

"Sure."

"What do you know about Ellis' father?"

"I only know that he's never been in his life. The one time I asked Sophia, she quickly brushed it off like she'd prefer not to talk about it. So, I left it alone. Why? Did something happen?"

I'm not sure if she wants anyone to know the details of what she told me in private. It's not my story to tell. So, I'll keep it short and to the point.

"Kenneth, Ellis' father, showed up at Sophia's house yesterday and surprised us all."

Dalton straightens in his seat, and his eyes widen. "What the fuck?"

"Yeah, my thoughts exactly." I turn my head to look out the window.

"Are Sophia and Ellis okay?"

"I don't know."

"What do you mean?"

I look back at him, unable to show any emotion at all. I truly am ruined, a broken shell of a man. "Sophia broke up with me. Asked *me* to leave. She chose him over me."

Dalton blows out a long breath. "It doesn't make sense. Sophia is crazy about you."

"I guess my promises and actions weren't enough to keep her."

"I've known you for a long time, Owen. You don't give up that easily. What's the deal with this Kenneth guy?"

"I've only met him once, but the way Soph talked about him...." I pause before I say too much. "Look, I don't trust him. I tried to get her to listen to reason, but she wouldn't. There was nothing I could do." *Not without harming her or Ellis.*

"So, that's it. You're just going to let them go?"

"Soph won't return any of my calls or texts. So, I'm going to respect her wishes."

Dalton doesn't seem happy with my answer, but he nods anyway. "She'll come around. Maybe when we return home, you'll talk things through and work it out."

I shrug. "Maybe," I agree, knowing it's highly unlikely that Sophia will. She seems to have made up her mind. "I just want to focus on work." *And try to forget about what I've lost.* "Can we do that?"

"Whatever you need." Dalton relents, but I know it won't be for long.

Twenty

Sophia

I cried myself to sleep last night.

I kept reading Owen's texts, listening to his voicemails, and my tears never failed me.

After Owen left Saturday, Kenneth was on his best behavior. He seemed satisfied with my sorrow and didn't try to stay or force any feelings out of me that weren't there. He focused most of his time on Ellis and promised to return to see him this morning before school.

It's Ellis' first day of school and should be a more exciting time, but Kenneth ruined that for me. He wasn't supposed to be the one wishing Ellis well.

The hardest part about all of this is Ellis asking where Owen had gone. I told him something had come up, and Owen had to leave earlier than expected. He also asked when Owen was returning, and I simply told him I didn't know.

As I stare at myself in the bathroom mirror, I notice that my eyes aren't as red and puffy as they feel. I thought about canceling my appointments and taking the day off, but I don't want Kenneth to get the wrong idea. Work is a blessing today, a distraction, and an escape from Kenneth.

I can't wait until he leaves town.

I groan into my palms, covering my face, then drop my hands to my belly full of anxiety. I give myself a once-over, then check on Ellis to see if he's ready.

My stomach clenches when the doorbell rings.

Kenneth never told me how he got past the gate, but my gut tells me it's him outside my door.

"You're here." I try to sound surprised when I open the door. "Come in." I step aside for him to enter before he takes it upon himself as he did the last time. "Ellis is in the kitchen finishing up breakfast."

"Thank you," Kenneth says, stepping inside.

I nearly choke on his words. I shot him a skeptical look. Whatever he's selling, I'm not buying it. I've fallen for his nice guy routine before, and look where that got me.

"We're leaving in ten minutes," I say matter-of-factly.

"We should talk, Jo. About what happens next." Kenneth takes two steps toward me and stops.

"You're right. We should." Because the only thing happening here is his relationship with Ellis. "But not today." I glance at the kitchen, hoping he will get a clue.

"I'm headed home after this for work, but I'll be back in a few days. We'll discuss your moving home then." Kenneth closes the distance between us, stopping in front of me.

My eyes widen, and I shake my head, no. He's too close, but that's the least of my worries because all I can focus on is what he said.

"My life, my job is here, Kenneth. Ellis is just starting school. I'm not moving."

Kenneth gently rubs his hand down my arm and leans in, pressing his lips to my temple. His breath crawls over my skin as he says, "We'll talk later." Then, he turns and walks toward the kitchen, leaving me speechless once again.

I pull myself together after a few minutes and follow him into the kitchen.

Kenneth is a different man around Ellis. He's the father I always wished Ellis had. But I have to remind myself that this is just one moment, a show. Real, but not lasting. Underneath his facade, there's still the same controlling beast he's always been.

"Alright, Bud. Time to go." I interrupt their conversation about sports, a topic Ellis knows next to nothing about.

Ellis rinses his bowl and sets it in the dishwasher.

Twenty-One

Owen

We've been on tour for two weeks, and I still haven't heard from Sophia. It's probably for the best, even though I haven't fully accepted that she's no longer mine.

I'm losing my mind. Anger is starting to outweigh my love for Sophia. It's hard to think of her now without seeing Kenneth next to her, touching her, holding her, kissing her, fucking her.

I grip the glass in my hand tighter, then throw it at the wall next to the tv. "Fuck!" I shout, my voice booming through the room. I stand, walking to the window, staring into the open sky. I grip my fingers behind my head, desperately wanting to forget.

Is this my life now, full of everything I'm used to but void of what matters most? I still have my family, but it's not the same. What Sophia and I had was on a whole other level, and it's getting harder to control my rage with each passing day.

A few seconds pass, and someone knocks on my bedroom door. I drop my hands, turning to look that way, then walk in that direction, glancing at the broken glass on the floor as I pass. I swing the door open full of frustration.

"You look like shit," Luke says, barging in and stopping next to the mess that I made. "Redecorating?" He raises a brow.

I shrug, leaving the door open and returning to the chair next to the bed. "Glass slipped out of my hand." My eyes move to the spot that I created on the wall. I'll have to pay for that, but it was worth it.

"What's going on with you, man?" Luke crosses the room, sitting on the window sill.

We spent the first half of our tour in Colorado and arrived in Emory, KY, last night for part two. Justin booked us this rental home for the duration of our visit so we'd be more comfortable. I've barely gotten any sleep, but not for lack of trying. It's hours before our performance tonight, and I don't know how I'll get through the empty time before then.

I look Luke's way, prepared to find humor in his expression, but there is none. He knows about the breakup. He knows heartache when he sees it because he's been through it himself. His grief and mine aren't the same, but pain is pain regardless of the intensity.

"I can't stop…." My voice cracks, and I pause, dragging my fingers through my hair.

I have to find a way to stop thinking.

"You should call her," Luke suggests.

"And say what?"

I miss her and Ellis like crazy.

I wish she had chosen me instead.

"She was clear about what she wanted, and that didn't include me." I drop my arm on the armrest.

"It's been weeks. Maybe Sophia's had a change of heart and doesn't know how to tell you." Luke tries to reason.

"Maybe Luke is right for once," Dalton says as he enters the room.

I tried laughing at his quip but failed miserably. "Or maybe he's wrong as usual." I chuckle sadly.

Dalton looks around the room until he notices my artwork on the floor and the wall. "Love what you've done with the place. Though, I'm not sure Justin will agree."

"I want to be the one to tell him." Luke jokes.

"He won't be happy for sure." I agreed.

"He will get over it. It's not the most expensive problem you've ever created." Dalton says. "Besides, you were due for a little trouble. I'm surprised you didn't break sooner."

Sophia broke me the moment she asked me to leave. I've just been holding it inside.

"You know what you need?" Luke asks, and I look at him.

Before Sophia, Luke's solution to all of my problems was to find someone to get under. I can't wait to hear what he thinks now.

"What?"

Luke crosses his arms over his chest. "A massage."

Dalton and I stare at him for a few silent seconds before breaking into laughter.

"A massage?" I give him a quizzical look.

"Don't knock it 'til you try it," Luke says.

"I see married life still suits you well," I say. "Do you enjoy the couples massage or singles?" I tease.

Luke shows me his middle finger, laughing. "Seriously though, you should try it. It helps."

"All kidding aside. Luke's idea isn't bad. It does help," Dalton agrees.

"Not you too," I mock.

Dalton shrugs.

Three hours later, we're all stretched out on massage tables in separate rooms, and I have to say, Luke and Dalton were right. Every muscle in my body is relaxed to the point where thinking doesn't hurt so bad.

I'm lying on my back with my eyes closed, thinking of Sophia—the way she would kiss me, her soft hands, her luscious body—and a quiet moan escapes me.

"I could take care of that for you," comes a voice in my ear.

My eyes fly open, and I glance down at my dick standing at attention underneath the sheet draped over me.

I look at my masseuse, Fiona. "Sorry. I don't know what came over me."

"No shame here," Fiona says. "Happens more than you'd think. As I said, I can handle that," she nods to my dick, biting her bottom lip.

I wonder if Luke meant this when he said I should try it.

I sit up, swinging my legs over the edge of the table. There was a time when I might have accepted Fiona's offer, but today, I'm just not ready. Sophia is still fresh on my mind, still whole in the pieces of my broken heart.

"Flattering, but I think I can manage." As I've done for the last two weeks.

"Are you sure? I'm very good at relieving stress and built-up pressure," Fiona tried again. She glances down at me once more, licking her lips.

"I'm sure you are." If her hands are any indication of what her mouth can do, she's probably one of the best, but the erection I'm sporting is not for her. I could close my eyes and pretend it was Sophia's mouth instead of hers. It's not like I haven't done it before Sophia and I got together, but it's different this time. I know what it's like to actually be with Sophia, and allowing another woman to pleasure me kind of feels like cheating.

"Look, Fiona, your offer is appealing, but I can't. I don't mix business with pleasure."

"Your loss." Fiona shrugs like it's not a big deal, but I catch a glimpse of hurt and anger on her face.

"I think it's safe to say we're done here." I tuck my dick back into the slit in my boxers and stand, letting the sheet fall to the floor.

Fiona packs her supplies, but I can feel her eyes on me as I slip on my shorts, leaving my chest bare. I watch as she leaves the room. Then, I plop down on the bed. She's a beautiful woman. A beautiful, willing woman. I can't believe I just passed up a free sprint to the finish line. I could've been sated by now, but instead, my balls are getting bluer by the minute.

I get up after a few minutes to take a shower. I imagine Sophia is here with me, and I rub one out while I'm in there.

· · · · · 𝅘𝅥 𝅘𝅥𝅮 𝅘𝅥𝅮 · · · · ·

Dalton, Luke, and I are in the dressing room after our performance when Joselyn and Rose pay them a surprise visit. It's not uncommon for them to sneak away from the kids for a day or two while we're on tour, but this time something feels off. I can't help but think that Sophia might have come with them if things hadn't taken a turn for the worse.

"We're going to head out, Owen," Dalton says, with Joselyn clinging to his side. "We'll meet you back at the house."

I know exactly what that means—a whole lot of everything is about to go down in that house, and I want no parts of it.

Luke and Rose got a head start already with their hands all over each other by the door.

"I'm going to grab a few drinks. Don't wait up," I tell them.

Rose takes a break from Luke's lips to look at me. "If you need us, call Justin." She wiggles her brows—which translates to exactly what she said—call Justin because she doesn't want to be disturbed.

Justin pops his head into the dressing room after they leave. I look up, assuming he wants to know what the hold-up is.

"Yeah?"

"There's a woman with a kid here to see you." Justin shoots me a questioning look.

I perk up, thinking it's Sophia and Ellis and Justin winds me back down in the next breath.

"She had this with her. Said you invited them." Justin holds a card in his hand that I recognize as one of ours.

"What does it say?" I ask to be sure.

"I.O.U. Free pass for Bonnie & Donald. OD."

"Let them in." I lean back on the couch again, not really in the mood for visitors, but a promise is a promise.

Bonnie and Donald enter the room, and I get a clearer view of them this time. Bonnie seems a little taller, which probably has something to do with her heels and the fact that she was standing behind a counter when I last saw her. Donald looks like he doesn't want to be here but plasters on a smile just the same.

"Bonnie, Donald, glad you could make it. Did you enjoy the show?" I ask, breaking out my showbiz persona. They didn't come here to see me sulk. They're expecting that guy they met in the grocery store a few weeks ago.

"Yeah," Donald says.

"I did," Bonnie chirps.

"How long are you in town?"

"Just the weekend. We flew in for the show. I figured we'd make it a mini-vacation." Bonnie grins. "And I'm glad we came. You guys really are something."

"Sorry, you missed the guys."

Bonnie waves her hand. "We'll catch them another time."

I tilt my head, looking at Donald, and he stares at me the same way. It seems like he wants to say something, but he doesn't.

"Well, since you're here for the night and I haven't eaten yet, why don't you join me for a late dinner?" My eyes move from Donald to Bonnie. I hadn't planned on going out to eat, but maybe they are just the thing to distract me for a while. "If you feel up to it."

"I would like that," Bonnie says, smiling sincerely.

Donald nods his agreement. "Do you know of any good burger joints?"

I smile, thinking, *a guy after my tastes.*

"No, but I'll check with our manager." Justin usually scouts for all the best places when we travel in case we want to go out.

I pull out my cell phone and call Justin even though he's right outside the door. I tell him what I want, and five minutes later, we're out the door.

There weren't many options to choose from, given it is almost midnight, but Justin did find a place with a little solitude—a quaint restaurant and bar that closes at 2:00 AM. We ordered as soon as we arrived, and Donald was mostly quiet during dinner as he chomped down on his burger and onion rings.

Bonnie is a chatterbox, asking questions, mostly about me and the guys—things that aren't personal and cast in the news. Talking to her is refreshing and easy like we're old acquaintances catching up.

"So, what did your lady friend think of the rose?" Bonnie asks as our time here nears the end. She eyes me curiously, waiting for my response.

She was like the cool aunt until that moment.

I swallow deeply, not expecting her question. A sad smile creeps onto my face as Sophia pops into my mind.

"She, she loved it," I stutter, my mind referring to that moment.

I wish I could go back to that day. I wish I had known now what she knew then.

Bonnie taps her fingers on the table, studying me. "Did I say something wrong?"

"No. It's nothing you said. Being away from Sophia is hard," I say truthfully without exposing the actual truth. "I try not to think about it."

"I shouldn't have pried," Bonnie says.

I spot Frank twirling his finger in the air by the bar out of the corner of my eye, signaling that it's time to go.

"Don't fret. It comes with the territory." I tell Bonnie. "We should get going before they kick us out."

I pay the tab, and we leave, stopping by Bonnie's hotel to drop her and Donald off.

The car stops, and Donald turns in the front passenger seat, looking back at me. "You're nothing like I thought you'd be. You're cool," he says.

"Thanks," I dragged out, confused by his statement.

Donald gets out of the car and ducks his head inside the door before closing it. "Mom, it's now or never," he says to Bonnie, who's sitting next to me, puzzling me further.

"I know," Bonnie says. "Go on inside. I just need a minute," She responds.

Donald leaves, and my first thought is that I've been entertaining a stalker all night, but Bonnie doesn't seem like a stalker. If she meant to do me harm, she wouldn't have brought her son, right? She didn't have to catch a plane to hurt me. I'm usually good at reading people. Did I peg her wrong?

"What's going on, Bonnie?" I ask with an air of caution.

"Owen, there's something you should know," Bonnie's eyes are fearful as she stares at me.

I don't like where this is going. The last time I heard those words was from Sophia's mouth, and nothing but heartache came after. I don't know why, but I let out a quiet laugh. I don't even have the energy to brace for Bonnie's response.

"Let me guess. You *are* a stalker," I joke because why not? It can't be worse than that. I've never met a known stalker before, but I think I could handle it if I did.

The light from the hotel front casts a dim glow around Bonnie's face in the dark, and she doesn't crack a smile. Her attention remains focused on me when she says, "I'm your mother, Owen."

I stare at her and do the only thing I can. I laugh because that can't be true. "Is this some kind of sick joke?"

Bonnie shakes her head. "It's not a joke. I *am* your mother."

My smile dims, and I catch Frank's eyes in the rearview mirror for a moment. I wonder briefly how much one heart can take before it stops working completely.

Bonnie's hands twist nervously on her lap as she continues to stare at me.

This time, I shake my head. "I think I would know if my parents were not my parents. They have pictures of us leaving the hospital. My dad and I have the same eyes," I defend.

"Owen," Bonnie tries, placing her hand over mine on my knee, and I shrug her off.

"Don't. I thought you were one of the good ones. Why did you come here? Why would you make up a lie like that?" I ask Bonnie.

Bonnie opens her mouth to say something, and I yell, "Get out! And stay the fuck away from me."

Bonnie blanches, her eyes widening into saucers.

"I think it's best if you go," Frank eyes Bonnie from the front seat, and she nods, scrambling for her purse.

I move my gaze away from her, staring straight ahead. What she claims can't be true. It can't.

I hear the door click open, and a heavy sigh follows. "If you ever want to know more, you know where to find me,"

Bonnie says. She gets out of the car and closes the door, yielding complete silence.

I prop my elbow on the side of the door, and as Frank drives away, I brace my forehead between my fingers, thinking about the hurricane that is my life.

Twenty-Two

Owen

I've let the idea of Bonnie being my mother simmer for two weeks so that I could focus on the rest of the tour. For two weeks, it's been pushed to the back of my mind. The moment my feet touched the ground in Cane, I allowed what Bonnie said to move to the forefront. I didn't mention it to the guys because I still don't believe it. Frank hasn't brought it up either.

I guess the only thing I can do when faced with a lie is to confront it. I walked away from Sophia without much of a fight. I won't shy away from this too.

While the guys went home to their families once we arrived, I had other plans. I needed answers that I knew my parents would never give me. So, I asked Frank to take me shopping, and now that I'm sitting outside Bonnie's store, I can't make my body move to go inside.

I watch as people come and go for over an hour as if somehow time will correct my irregular heartbeats, and Frank waits patiently with me.

"Do you think she may be telling the truth?" I ask Frank, and he looks at me.

"There's only one way to find out." Frank glances at the store and back at me. "Do you need me to run interference? I could go inside and ask her to come out or meet you somewhere more private."

"That would probably be best. I don't know what I was thinking coming here."

"I get it." Frank shrugs. "You want to hear both sides, and since Bonnie came to you first, it's only natural to want to hear from her first."

I ponder Frank's words and the truth within them. If Bonnie hadn't said anything, there would be nothing to question. So, I owe it to myself to hear what she has to say—whether it's true or false—before I face my parents.

I give Frank an amenable nod. "Could you ask her to come out?"

"Sure." Frank moves to get out of the car.

"Wait," I tell him, scanning my surroundings. "I'll go inside. It will appear less suspicious and more like a business exchange."

Frank smiles like a proud papa.

I square my shoulders, inhaling and exhaling a calming breath before getting out of the car. Frank follows me inside.

Donald is behind the register again, and he does a double-take when I enter. The calm, approving expression he gave me when I saw him last is gone. He looks angry with me, but I can't think about him. It's between his mother and me.

I come face to face with Donald, and he doesn't give me a chance to speak.

"Are you back to finish her off?" Donald asks in an unsettled quiet tone.

I stuff my hands into my pockets to keep from snatching him up. I get that he's angry. I admire him for defending his mother, but I am not the bad guy here.

"I just want answers," I say calmly.

Donald lets out a snarky grin. "Mom tried to give them to you, but you wouldn't listen. Do you know how hard it was for her to come to you? How hard it was watching her deal with losing you again?"

I open my mouth and close it when he keeps talking.

"No, you don't because you don't care about anyone but you," Donald huffs.

That's not true. I shake my head.

"Maybe I was right about you all along. You're an insensitive, entitled prick, just like all the rest of them," Donald accuses.

My head turns to the side, hearing a harsh intake of air.

Bonnie comes rushing behind the counter. "That's enough, Donald," she whisper-shouts.

"But, Mom," Donald tries.

"No buts. Have some respect," Bonnie scolds.

Donald clamps his mouth shut.

I'm still stuck on what Donald said. I don't think I've ever been called either of those things. Well, not to my face. However, I think I deserve to be a little insensitive in this case.

Frank nudges my shoulder with his shoulder, nodding behind us and reminding me where we are.

I looked behind me, thankful that no one was close enough to hear our conversation. Then, I turn back to face Bonnie. I examine her features to see if they resemble mine in any way, but it's hard to tell because I don't want it to be true. I would much rather this be a joke, but something about how she looks at me tells me that it's not.

"Is there somewhere we can talk?" I ask Bonnie.

"Mom," Donald places his hand over Bonnie's on the counter, and she looks at him, covering his hand with hers.

"I'll be fine." Bonnie pats his hand. When her eyes return to mine, she nods her head toward the door that she came out of. "Follow me."

I follow Bonnie into a small office while Frank remains outside. She offers me the seat in front of her desk, and I take it, jumping straight into conversation.

"Now that I've had time to cool off, I'm ready to listen. So, how are *you*, my mother?"

Bonnie sighs, taking the seat next to me, but she doesn't look at me. She stares straight ahead.

"I was nineteen years old when I met your mother. I had just started my break when Sara came in with a glum look on her face. On her way out, I asked her if she was okay, and for some reason, I can't explain, she confided in me. Sara said she and your father had tried everything to have a child, and nothing worked. I asked her if she'd thought about surrogacy, and she responded that the idea frightened her. When we were done talking, she thanked me for listening, and we parted on that thought."

Bonnie takes a deep breath; her gaze still fixed forward.

"Imagine my surprise when a few weeks later, Sara came back to ask me if I would be the one. If I would carry their child. At first, I said no. I couldn't imagine giving up a child that I carried for nine months, but in the end, I agreed."

Bonnie pauses, placing her hands over her belly as if she remembers what it feels like to be pregnant.

"The day you were born was one of the hardest of my life." Bonnie finally turns to look at me. "I remember staring into your tiny eyes and the feel of your small hands wrapped around my pinkie. I couldn't stop crying. I didn't want to let you go."

"Why did you?" I ask as if it was just that simple.

Bonnie smiles sadly. "Because you were as much theirs as you were mine, even more so. Because I made a promise.

I let you go without a fight, and I intended to honor my word, but Sara and Andrew never gave me a chance. They took out a restraining order, and I wasn't allowed contact with you. I was forced to secretly watch you grow up from afar, but I've thought about you every day."

I stare at Bonnie, trying to process what she's told me. I feel like she's telling the truth. She can't be that emotional and not be telling the truth unless she's a psycho. And I don't think she is. There is one thing that doesn't add up, though.

"Why come to me now? What do you have to gain?" I ask sincerely.

"I would've stayed away forever, Owen. But when you walked into my store, I saw it as a sign that we were meant to meet. And you, inviting us to your show, sealed it. It wasn't my intention to disrupt your life. I don't expect anything. Finally, getting to meet and talk with you is more than I deserve."

Bonnie clears her throat, wiping away a lone tear that slips down her cheek. Then she places her hand on my arm.

"You're a fine young man, Owen. Your parents should be proud." She pats my arm gently then drops her hand back into her lap.

I don't know what to say or how to feel about any of this. Bonnie and I had this connection from the moment we met, and now I know why. My parents have kept it a secret my whole life while pushing me away. They never intended for me to find out, but life has taught me that secrets don't stay hidden.

"Thank you," I tell Bonnie. "For telling me the truth."

"Sure. If you ever want to know anything or need anything, I'm here," Bonnie says.

I didn't apologize for my anger when she first told me. She should've expected me to react. I leave her office with the explanation I came for and a little more clarity—enough to confront my parents.

I stop at the register to call a truce with Donald on the way out. "We should hang out sometime." I give him a slip of paper with my number on it. I can't believe I have a brother. It's new territory, and he probably hates me, but that can change.

Donald stares at me with a mix of awe and confusion, saying nothing at all. He does slip the paper into his pocket. I take that as a sign of good faith.

"Well, I hope to hear from you." I rap my knuckles on the countertop, then leave.

· · · · · ♩ ♪ · · · · ·

I drop my things in my small space over the garage and walk to the main house.

I'm angry with my parents, but I don't want to be disrespectful. We've been getting along so well lately, and regardless of what they kept from me, they are still my parents. I may not be the best me I can be, but I am who I am because they raised me. My life could've been different, better or worse, but I'll never know.

Mom is sitting outside on the porch swing. She glances up at me as I approach. "You're home," she says excitedly.

I try to smile, but I think it falls flat instead. Mom poses her cheek, and I lean down when I reach her, placing a peck on it.

"Is Dad around?" I sit next to her, feeling conflicted.

"He's in his office." Mom nods toward the house.

Dad spent a lot of time in his office during my childhood. Now I'm wondering if that was to avoid me too.

"Do you think he would mind if I interrupted?" Dad always told me not to bother him in his office.

Mom looks at me, squinting her eyes and tilting her head. "Is something wrong?"

I don't answer that because everything in my life is wrong at the moment. I left in turmoil and came back even worse than before.

"I need to talk to both of you. It'll be better that way."

Mom is quiet for a moment, watching me as if she's trying to figure out what it could be.

"Okay. It's obviously important, so I'm sure your father won't mind. Is this about Sophia?"

The mention of Sophia's name causes my heart to stutter. "I'll talk as soon as Dad is present."

Mom pats my knee twice then stands. "I'll get him. Come inside."

I follow Mom inside, splitting from her to go into the living room while she gets Dad. I sat on the edge of the sofa with my elbows on my knee, and my head hung low. The seconds seem to tick by in slow motion as I wait, but my heart is racing at the speed of lightning. I'm still not sure how to begin the conversation.

"What's this I hear about a wedding?"

I look up, hearing Dad's voice flow through the room. There's an unusual smile on his face like he's happy for me.

A wedding? He thinks I'm getting married. And he's joking about it.

Sophia and I are far from marriage. We are far from anything at this point. She won't even return my calls.

"Definitely not a wedding," I responded.

"Well," Dad sits in his usual spot in the double recliner. "If it's not a wedding, then what else could be so pressing?"

How about the fact that you omitted the truth my entire life?

"Is this about the tour?" Mom asks curiously, sitting next to Dad.

"Not entirely."

Two sets of eyebrows rise as they stare at me.

"It was an experience I'll never forget." I continued. "I ran into some interesting people." I hold my head higher, leaning back on the sofa.

"How is that pressing?" Dad asks.

"Funny you should ask that because one of those people claimed to be my mother."

Dad chokes on a cough, and Mom gasps.

"What exactly did this woman say?" Mom asks, and I shoot her an incredulous stare.

Of all the ways she could have responded, that is what she came up with? I kind of expected her to lie and say that it was not true, but she didn't.

"She had quite the story to tell—one that I refused until I returned home today." My eyes swivel between them, gauging their reactions.

Dad's mouth is pressed into a hard line, and his eyes are full of fury.

"And you believe her?" Mom asks.

I shrug. "Can you think of a reason why I shouldn't?"

"You don't even know the woman," Mom says, and I strain my eyes to look at her.

"I know that she didn't lie to me—at least not about being my mother."

"Watch your tone, Son," Dad warns.

My eyes move to him. I hadn't realized I raised my voice. My chest heaves angrily, my arms crossed over my chest, and my hands are painfully gripping my sides.

"You're angry," Dad states the obvious. "But that doesn't give you an excuse to forget who you are and who you're talking to."

"Who am I?" I chuckle. "Because all this time, I thought I knew."

"Oh, Owen." Mom sighs. "Whether we share the same blood or not, you *are* my son." She glances at Dad and back to me. "Our son. You don't know what it's like to have a child and have to worry about that child being taken away from you at any moment."

I feel like I've already lost a son with Ellis, but I leave that out of this.

"You have to understand," Dad chimes in. "Sara was terrified of losing you, and I would've done anything to take that fear away. So, I ensured that Bonnie wouldn't be a threat, and I'm not sorry I did it. I would've done anything in my power to ease Sara's worries—to keep you both safe."

I release my arms, bringing my hands up to rub the space between my eyebrows and hairline, before dropping my hands to my thighs.

My eyes meet Dad's again. "Is that the real reason you kept me at arm's length? Because being around me reminded me of what you'd done?"

"Yes and no," Dad answers vaguely.

"Then why have a child if you couldn't love him with your whole heart?" I rebut, not satisfied with his reply.

Dad blows out a long breath. "Loving you was never the problem, Owen. I loved you long before you were born. It was the fear of losing you that kept me away. Even though we had taken every precaution, there was still a chance that Bonnie could waltz back into your life."

"That was never Bonnie's intention," I say a bit more calmly.

"How can you sit there and defend a woman you've only known for five minutes?" Mom asks angrily. "She will tell you anything to make herself appear like a saint in all of this. The *only* reason she didn't come for you is that she didn't have the choice." Tears fill her eyes, but she refuses to let them fall.

Dad reaches over the armrest to hold her hand.

"Bonnie had plenty of chances to come to me after the restraining order was lifted, but she never did, and she never would have if I hadn't shown up at her store."

My parent's eyes widen, and Dad's hand grips the arm of the recliner.

"We never meant for you to find out like this," Mom says. "We were going to tell you when you came home."

"You want to know what I think?" Neither one of my parents answered. So, I keep talking. "I think that you never meant for me to find out at all. I think it's why you hated my career choice and why you frowned on my relationship with Sophia." I swallow deeply after Sophia's name falls from my mouth.

Mom balks, but she can't deny my accusations, and neither can Dad.

"What do you want from us, Son?" Dad asks sullenly.

What do I want?

What's done is done. There's nothing that will change the way things are. I shake my head, close my eyes for a few seconds, then look back at them.

"I'm sorry, Owen." Mom brushes her fingers under her eyes.

The anger I felt toward them simmers down a little with her words, leaving a nagging ache.

"I understand your need to keep me safe. I get why you did it. But what hurts the most is that you didn't trust that I could handle the truth. I wish you had just told me. You are my parents. I never would've abandoned you for someone I barely know," I say, my voice cracking on the last word.

"What can we do to make it right?" Dad asks.

"That's the thing. We, this family, were never wrong. Bonnie gave you a gift, and you gambled away a relationship with your son that could've been so much better than this." I motion between us.

A few seconds of silence pass, then I stand to leave because there's nothing left to say.

"I need some time to myself." I walk past them, and Mom stands. Her mouth opens, but no sound filters out.

Once I'm back inside my small apartment, my thoughts drift to Sophia. I think about every conversation we had the week before I left, dissecting them one by one. There were signs that I missed, signaling that we'd end up this way, but I was blinded by love. Maybe if I hadn't held back, if I had pushed harder for answers, I could've helped before it was too late.

Is it too late, though?

I know that I walked away and said I'd let Sophia go, but I don't feel it. The urge to have her is not gone. There's still more fight left in me. I have to convince her that there's still a chance and that Ellis will be okay. Kenneth may have connections, but so do I. I won't let Sophia throw us away because of him.

Twenty & Three

Sophia

Sophia, please answer the phone. We need to talk.

It's been nearly a month since Owen's last contact, days longer since I've seen him.

I miss him.

I think about him, and my heart breaks daily.

I re-read his messages, and my temperature rises every time.

I listen to his voicemails every night, my stomach flutters, and I cry.

And after all that time—when I thought he'd forgotten about me and moved on—he sends another message.

And my stomach flutters, and I cry.

It's taking everything I am to be strong, and Owen goes and does it again. As if I don't have enough to deal with already.

Thankfully Kenneth has a job, so he's not around during the week. He's been here every single weekend, though, and even that's too much. He rents a hotel not far away when he visits because I refuse to let him stay. He keeps pressuring me about moving *home,* and I keep telling him that this *is* my home. I think Ellis being in school helps a lot, but I know there will come a time when even that won't matter.

I can feel Kenneth's patience running thin when he speaks to me, his unsettled tone and strict posture. Every time he comes close to me, I want to scream. Every time he touches my arm or brings my hands to his lips, I want to punch him like he used to do to me. If he ever tried to kiss me, I probably would without thinking.

I still don't understand Kenneth, and I doubt that I ever will. How can he be so sweet and nurturing with Ellis and encompass such dark intentions for me all at once?

This moment—as I sit on the back porch, staring at Ellis and Kenneth throw the football back and forth—is one of the rarest. I find a semblance of peace, and a smile creeps onto my face because my son seems happy.

"Hey, Jo, why don't you come join us," Kenneth's voice travels across the yard, and I cringe.

My eyes flit to him, keeping my smile intact, but the emotion behind it sours. "Some other time," I yell back, returning my gaze to Ellis. Ellis waves and I wave back. Then they return to tossing the ball.

About thirty minutes later, Ellis hurries past me, saying he has to pee, leaving me alone on the porch with Kenneth.

Kenneth stares down at me, holding his hand out. "I know what you need," he says.

My eyes drop to his hand and travel back up to his eyes.

I know what I need too, and it's not you.

I just stare at him, keeping my thoughts to myself.

"Come on, Jo. It's been a month. When are you going to warm up to me?"

I don't know. NEVER!

"I've been patient and kind, considering," Kenneth has the nerve to say.

You've been kind before.

I continue to stare at him, and he finally drops his hand, sitting next to me instead. He puts his arm behind me over the back of the chair, and my body tenses. I hate that I react that way to him after all the time that has passed. I'm stronger than that, but there's always going to be that one percent that braces for the blow.

"I want us to go back to the way things used to be, Jo."

He can't be serious. I turned my head to look at him, remembering just how bad things had gotten between us. Does he not remember, or does he not care?

An ounce of courage bubbles up inside of me. "You hurt me, Kenneth, over and over again, and I never want to go back to that place."

"We can start fresh. I've changed, Jo. You'll see." Kenneth's arm touches the shirt on my back, and his hand lands on my shoulder, his thumb rubbing small circles there.

It's not the first time Kenneth has said those lines to me. I recall those moments when I didn't have the power to say no, and we'd start the cycle of ruin all over again—the moments where I thought, *this time will be different. This time I can help him.* The script is so vivid and familiar that I know what's coming next.

"Remember the long walks we would take around the park? How we would hold hands and plan our future?" Kenneth smiles at me. "Those were some of the best times of my life," he adds as if it's something to celebrate.

"Yeah, they were good times," I agree. "But they never erased the moments that got us there. I won't be your punching bag anymore, Kenneth."

Kenneth's thumb stops moving, and something akin to shame washes over his face, but only briefly. Then, his nostrils flare. His hands tighten on my shoulder, and anger takes over.

"There you are," I say boldly.

Kenneth lifts his other hand so fast that I barely see it moving toward my face, but before it connects, the back door flies open, and Ellis appears. The smack that I had expected turned to a gentle palm on my cheek.

I'm speechless but not shocked at all.

"Can I have something to eat?" Ellis asks.

I give Ellis my attention. "Sure, Bud. Your dad was just leaving," I announced, pulling out of Kenneth's grip to stand.

"Jo," Kenneth says sweetly, grabbing my wrist as if the last few seconds hadn't happened.

"Don't." I pull away from him and follow Ellis inside with Kenneth right behind us. I walk directly to the front door, open it, and step aside for Kenneth to go.

Kenneth stops in front of Ellis and me. His brows bunch as he displays a devious smile of warning.

I swallow hard and hold my head high. He may have forced Owen out of my life, but that doesn't mean that I want him.

Kenneth drops his eyes to Ellis. "I'll see you next week, Big Guy."

"Do you have to go?" Ellis asks, and Kenneth glances at me, but I don't relent. I don't mind being the bad guy.

"Dad has some things to take care of," I cut in.

"I'm afraid your mom's right," Kenneth agrees. "But I will be back," he says pointedly, his eyes rising to meet mine again. "Later, Jo." His hands brush down my arm before he walks out.

I close the door like a sane human being instead of slamming it behind him as I did in my mind.

I smile pleasantly at Mr. & Mrs. Hensley as they exit my office Monday morning. They are old clients who came in to update their records, and I'm glad they're leaving. Not because I don't like them. I do. I just needed a break, and they were my last clients before noon.

I close the door once they're gone and walk over to my desk. As soon as I sit down, Maggie opens the door and pokes her head inside.

"Hey. I'm taking you out for lunch today," Maggie says.

I rarely leave the office for lunch, and this is one of those days where I'm not feeling it. I just want to close my blinds, lock the door, lie down on my couch, and take a nap, or at the very least try to.

"I don't think so, Maggie."

Maggie swings the door wide open and steps inside. She walks toward me like she's on a mission and pulls me up out of my chair. "I'm not taking no for an answer. You think I haven't noticed you moping around here for weeks?"

I open my mouth to object.

"Well, I have, and it ends today," Maggie continues. "So, you're going whether you want to or not."

News about Kenneth being Ellis' father is everywhere, but no one knows that Owen and I split up except our family. Maggie probably thinks my moping had to do with Owen being gone for the past month, and I guess that's part of it. But there's an even bigger part that she doesn't know.

Maggie grabs my purse and my wrist, dragging me out of my office, and I don't have the energy to stop her.

Every eye in the office is on me as I walk through. It's normal but a little weird, too, because of the added expressions and gestures. Almost everyone is standing, which is not normal at all. A few women have their hands over their hearts, and the men's faces are a mix of impressed and…. Annoyed? I can't tell.

"This is going to be great," Maggie says next to me. We reach the door, and she opens it for me to exit first.

I'm thoroughly confused by everyone when I step outside. Lights flash from somewhere in the distance. I take a few more steps, stopping when my eyes land on Owen. My heart beats in all of the ways it's not supposed to, and I forget how to breathe.

Owen is standing in front of a slick black SUV with dark tinted windows. His hair is brushed back, and he's wearing black jeans and a charcoal gray shirt that's buttoned halfway. His guitar hangs around his neck with his fingers at the ready. When he sees me, he smiles that smile that I love so much. Then he strikes a chord that shoots straight through me. He looks like my Owen wrapped up in a rock star.

I finally release a breath, and another, and another, and after a few seconds, I look like every woman inside the office. My eyes are glossy, and both of my hands are on my chest.

Owen strikes another chord and another until it becomes the sweetest unsung melody I've ever heard. I've heard him play during practice, but never like this. And if that weren't enough, he begins to sing as he walks toward me.

My knees get weaker with every step he takes, with every flick of his wrist, with every lyric he voices.

Owen reaches me, ending his song with, "My Melody."

I still can't speak, but I'm sure I will fall if someone doesn't catch me. My legs turn to jello, but I don't hit the ground.

"I've got you," Owen's arms wrap around my back as he whispers in my ear, and I melt into his arms.

All reasonable thought disappears as Owen holds me. He steadied my body, and when I could stand on my own, his hands cupped my face, and he kissed me.

And I kiss him back.

Twenty-Four

Owen

Silence drowns out the world around Sophia and me for a few seconds. Her tongue slides against mine, and I release a quiet, greedy moan. My arm tightens around her back, and I pull her closer. Our kiss slows to a crawl, then a torturous stop. I touch my forehead to hers. Our breaths are frantic, mixing with the still humid air. The world spins swiftly around us then stops. The flashing lights and noise return, and I remember where we are.

Sophia fists my shirt in her hands with her eyes lowered to my chest. "Owen," she whispers in a pained voice.

I raise my head, bringing my finger to her chin, and tilting her head up. "Soph."

The look in her eyes hurts. She wants us, I felt it in our kiss, but she's conflicted. I need to take her away from here to talk in private.

"You're taking the rest of the day off." I stare into Sophia's glossy eyes, and she shakes her head, no.

"I can't just leave, Owen," she objects.

I look over Sophia's shoulder at Maggie, who's a few feet away. I spoke to her this morning about my plans to pick Sophia up, and she jumped on board.

I wave Maggie over, and she comes, giving Sophia her purse. "Have fun," she says giddily.

Sophia looks at Maggie. "I have clients."

"You *had* one client," Maggie corrects. "They've been rescheduled. So, please, get into this man's ride before I do," Maggie teases.

"What about my car?" Sophia asks.

"It will be here when I drop you off in the morning," I jump in. There's no way I'm spending tonight without her.

Sophia clamps her mouth shut, all out of excuses.

"Thanks, Maggie." I nod her way, then grab Sophia's hand and guide her to the Yukon.

Frank raises the privacy glass once Sophia and I are settled in the back. Silence engulfs us as the truck begins to move.

Sophia gazes at me like I've done one thousand things right and one thousand things wrong, but I'm not sorry that I came for her, that I'm willing to fight for us. How can I be when she's finally close enough for me to touch? Why would I be when she's everything that I want? The only thing I'm sorry about is leaving things the way I did.

"I know what you're thinking, Soph." I lace my fingers through hers.

"You do?"

"You're thinking, I shouldn't have come, and there's no way this will work."

Sophia gives a half-smile. "Still a wise man, I see."

"But I'm right where I need to be, where you want me to be." I pause. "Tell me I'm wrong. Tell me you don't want to be here with me right now."

Sophia swallows as the small smile slips from her face. She looks away from me. "We can't be together, Owen. I won't risk it. I can't," she says on a shaky breath.

"I won't accept that. I won't allow you to throw your life away for someone who hurt you. I can help you, Soph. I'll help you fight for Ellis. No judge would take a child away from their mother without good reason, and you are a wonderful mother."

"Owen," Sophia sighs, gazing at the dark window in front of her.

"My father can help. He's never lost a case."

"Your father barely tolerates me. What makes you think he'd help?"

"I know he will." My mind flashes to the truth that unfolded only days ago. My parents would do anything to make me happy right now, to try and make up for their omission. "He wants me to be happy, and *you* make me happy, Soph." I leave out the part where he thought Sophia and I were getting married.

Sophia shakes her head. "You have to let this go. You have to let me go." She refuses to look at me still.

I turn slightly in the seat, bringing my finger to her chin, and guide her gaze back to mine. "That is not an option. I won't ever let you go again. We've only been apart for one month, and it nearly drowned me. Pain was the force that got me through, but I don't want to be driven by pain, Soph. I want to be moved by love. I want what we have to be my strength. Don't you want that too?" I search her eyes, finding my answer clear as day, but I need her to say it—to tell me I'm not the only one willing to fight. "Nothing will happen to Ellis or you." I drop my hand to hers on her lap.

Sophia stares back at me, and I hate that the tears in her eyes stem from fear. "It's not Ellis or myself that I'm worried about," she says.

"Then who? Wait." I scrunch my brows. "Kenneth threatened you with me?"

"I love you too much to lose you completely, Owen." Sophia brings her palm to my cheek. "I would rather you *live* a normal life without me than something happen to you while with me, knowing I could've prevented it."

My heart thrums in my chest. I don't deserve Sophia's sacrifice. "I don't want normal. I want you and Ellis and all of the chaos that comes with it." I brush her hair behind her ear with my finger. "You let me deal with Kenneth. He won't do anything stupid."

"But what if he does?"

I shrug. "I'll handle it. This is not on you. Understand?"

"I can't lose you, Owen."

"You won't." I tap my thighs. "Now, come here."

Sophia hesitates for a moment, unsure. Then, she hikes her dress up and straddles me, placing her forehead against mine, our breaths mingling. I palm her ass, pulling her closer to me, a surprised yelp leaving her mouth. Her hands rest on my shoulders as she settles.

Sinking myself deep into Sophia should be the last thing on my mind, but I can't keep the thought away with her warmth pressed against me. My lips gravitate to hers, pressing sweetly, then firmly. I try to pull away, but she stops me, bringing our lips back together, deepening the kiss. She kisses me with an urgency like never before. She wants me just as bad, but is it because she's starved, or just starved for me?

Those thoughts I had about Sophia and Kenneth while I was away flashed like memories in my head. We were broken up. If she had sex with him, I would have to accept it. I don't have the right to ask, but I need to know.

I pull away from her lips to look at her. "Did he? Did you?" I try, but the words won't come out. It hurts thinking about it, but it pains me even more to say them.

But Sophia gets it. "No." She holds my face. "No," she says again.

My cock swells even more beneath her, drawing a smile from her.

"How much time do we have?" Sophia asks.

"How much time do you need?" Because I don't need long at all.

I guess she doesn't need long either.

I raise my hands, surrendering, as Sophia scoots back to unbutton my jeans. I pull them down a fraction, freeing myself. I palm my dick, holding it steady as Sophia positions herself over me. She lowers slowly onto me, and I grip her waist, watching her. I draw my bottom lip into my mouth as she conforms to my girth. The familiarity and pleasurable sensation heat my skin, jars my senses.

Sophia moans as I push further inside of her, meeting her wall. One hand is at the back of my neck, fingers biting my skin, and the other gripping my shoulder as she finds her rhythm.

The sound of the music rises over the smooth rumble of the engine, reminding me that we're not alone. But it doesn't matter that we've been found out. All that matters at this moment is us.

Our lips meet again in a slow dance, matching our actions. Sophia rides me like a pro-slow, fast, warped, then slow again. Her hips gyrate over me, and I lift my hips to meet her. We're in sync as if we'd never been apart. I whimper from sheer pleasure. I actually whimpered.

"Fuck, Soph." She takes every inch of me in with every single stroke, driving me wild, making me want more, and feeling the urge to let go all at once.

Sophia takes a breath, and I pepper kisses across her jawline to her neck, dipping my head lower, pinching her nipple between my lips.

"Mmm," Sophia moans, her head tipping back. "Yes." She begins to move faster, her core tightening around me, coaxing me to the edge along with her.

I try to hold back, not wanting it to be over, but she feels too good, so wet, so tight. Her moans are like music to my ear. I want to bask in her love and let go.

My eyes close, and a coarse growl leaves me as I take the final plunge inside her, dropping my head to the back of the seat and clutching her thighs.

I open my eyes when I feel Sophia's lips on my chin. She bites down teasingly, letting out a tiny giggle.

"I've missed you, Owen Daye. You are worse than a drug." Sophia nips at my chin again.

"You make it sound like a bad thing." I chuckle drunkenly.

Sophia kisses me shortly, then moves to sit next to me. "It's a very bad thing, but a very good, bad thing." She pulls a few wipes from her purse, handing two to me.

I clean and recompose myself. "Well, that's perfect because you're not getting rid of me." I pull her to my side, wrapping my arm around her back.

"Now that you've kidnapped me in front of the entire office, and possibly the whole world, where are you taking me?" Sophia looks over at me.

"Well, the plan was to get you in here and just drive, turn on the charm, and grovel until you took me back."

Sophia grins. "Well, that didn't take long."

"What can I say. I'm easy. You're easy. We're easy for each other." I smirk. "I told Frank I would knock when I was ready to stop."

Sophia blushes. "Do you think he heard us?"

"Doesn't matter." I kiss her temple. Frank's a cool guy. It's not the first time he's had to mask our actions.

"And now that we've acknowledged my slutty behavior?" Sophia raises her eyebrows.

"I'm taking you to lunch as Maggie promised. Then, we're going to visit my father."

Sophia sucks in a breath as if she's just remembered something. "I have to get Ellis from school."

"Dalton has you covered."

"You've thought of everything." Sophia covers her face with her hands for a few seconds, then drops them to her lap. "I've made such a mess of things." She sighs.

"You did what you thought was best."

"Your dad...." Concern outlines her features.

"My dad," I say, still not over my recent discovery, "has done things to protect his family too." Saying it out loud and thinking about Sophia's situation, I understand the need to protect a little more. I probably would've behaved similarly, if not the same. I just want Sophia and Ellis to be safe, whatever it takes.

"I'll never be able to repay you for this." Sophia holds the hand in my lap. Her tone still houses a hint of worry.

"Loving me is enough. It will always be enough."

· · · · · ♪ ♪ · · · · ·

Sophia and I grabbed a couple of hot dogs earlier and went back to my place, where I texted Dad to ask if we could talk when he got home. Now, we're sitting on my parent's couch across from Dad again, having a stare down.

I haven't told Sophia about my issue. I thought it was best to wait with everything she's going through. I also haven't told Dad why we're here. I haven't spoken to him or mom since I confronted them Saturday. So, he's probably wondering why now, and why bring Sophia to bear witness?

Dad's arms are resting on the arms of the recliner. His eyes are dark—matching the black suit he's wearing—and curious. For as long as I can remember, Dad had always spoken first when it came to me. But today, he's quiet, waiting for my opening statement.

"I need your help, Dad. Sophia needs your help."

Sophia and I discussed the best way to present her case to my father over lunch and decided it was best to do it together. She wanted me with her.

Dad tilts his head slightly, lifting an eyebrow and focusing his gaze on Sophia. "How can I help?"

Twenty-Five

Sophia

Andrew is good. Very good. I've only met Owen's father once and have never researched any of his cases, but I know somehow. Even in the comfort of his own home, he has this pride about him. He exudes confidence, and it's a little intimidating, but I hold my head high and stare back at him.

I know that Andrew doesn't hate me. I also know that he would've chosen differently for his son if the choice were his. But I don't let him know that it bothers me, that I care what he thinks, even though I would very much like his approval.

I almost expect him to tell me to get lost, find someone else. I'm surprised when Andrew asks, *"How can I help?"*

I push the negative thoughts to the back of my mind and take a deep breath because this meeting isn't about Owen and me. I hold Owen's hand as I explain the situation to his dad. Andrew's gaze never falters, and not once does his expression show judgment as I speak. I'm thankful for that.

Owen gives my hand a gentle squeeze when I'm done, but it does little to calm my tension. Still, I'm glad he's offering his support.

"So, what are my options?" I return Andrew's gaze.

Andrew's jaw ticks as he straightens in his seat. His eyes roam from me to Owen and back to me, making the source of his frustration unclear. I hope he doesn't fault Owen for dropping my mess in his lap. Owen's life was good until he met me.

Andrew clears his throat. "The good news is, there's no chance of you losing your son. The bad news," Andrew pauses. "Kenneth could petition for joint custody once paternity is established. And since there's no proof of abuse, he may get it."

My forehead draws together. I had already assumed as much, but it still hurts to hear it from the law.

"Are you worried that Kenneth could harm Ellis?" Andrew asks.

I consider the question. Kenneth has been kind to Ellis since they met. I don't think he would hurt him, but I can't be sure. The worst outcome I imagined was Kenneth trying to take Ellis away from me completely for spite.

"I don't know." I glance at Owen.

Andrew nods. "To protect everyone involved," he glances at Owen and back, "I would advise supervised visits with Ellis through an outside party and increased security at home until this is sorted out. If things should escalate before or after then, get a restraining order. Any misstep on Kenneth's part decreases his chances of winning custody of any kind."

"So, you'll take my case?"

"I would do anything to protect my family." Andrew looks at Owen. An understanding passes between them, and Owen nods, smiling tightly. "So, yes. I'll take your case."

"Thanks, Dad."

"Thank you." I let out a breath of relief.

"My pleasure. I've gone against guys like Kenneth before, and it won't be easy, but I think you have a shot at keeping full custody if this goes to court. His type always slips up." Andrew flashes a confident smile, leaning forward in his seat, his hands slapping the armrest as he does. "Come by my office tomorrow, and I'll set things in motion. And don't worry about the cost. This one's on me." Andrew stands.

"Yes, Sir. Thanks again."

Owen and I stand with him. I want to give Andrew a great big hug, but he doesn't seem like the type. So, I just stand there with a grateful smile on my face instead.

"Are you kids staying for dinner?" Andrew asks.

I open my mouth to respond, but Owen beats me to it.

"Not tonight. We have to pick Ellis up from Dalton's."

Something is hovering between them that I can't decipher.

Andrew moves his gaze to me. "I'll see you tomorrow then."

"Tomorrow," I agree.

Owen seems to be holding his breath until we exit the house. When we get into his car, I have to ask. "What was that about?"

"What?" Owen pulls onto the road, looking straight ahead.

"That weird exchange between you and your dad."

Owen reaches across the armrest, places his hand on my knee, and squeezes gently before returning his hand to the wheel. "I just want to focus on you right now, okay."

"No. That's not how this works. You came back for me and all of my curiosity. This relationship can't be all about me. I know something else is bothering you. So, tell me. I can be your healer too."

A deafening pause falls between us. Owen sighs and glances at me, then focus back on the road.

"This is going to sound strange, but the owner of Packard's grocery is my mother."

I gasp. "Your."

"Mother. Yes, I know." Owen finished my sentence.

"How is that possible?" I don't know Owen's parents well, but I have eyes. He and his father are not identical, but their relation is evident.

"The store owner, Bonnie, is my surrogate mother." Owen shrugs. "It's not a big deal."

"From where I'm sitting, it seems like it is."

"It's not. My parents aren't the first to hire a surrogate."

"What's the problem then?"

Owen has been so patient with me. It's only right that I return the sentiment. I wait, watching his expression hover between calm understanding and anger.

"I never understood my parents—not the way they treated me, and certainly not the way they loved me. I believed that I was the problem, and they never corrected me. They questioned every choice I've ever made, including you." Owen glances my way. "But it was all for selfish reasons. Everything they've done was meant to keep me from a truth that was bound to come out. You probably think I'm overreacting, but it hurts that I heard it from a stranger at one of the lowest points in my life."

Guilt punches me in my chest, and I turn away from him. You never know what the next person is going through unless they tell you, and even then, you still don't know. I wonder if he has anything else bottled up.

I despise Kenneth with a passion, but Owen's words ring true to my life, too, except I'm the culprit. I'm the keeper of secrets. Sure, I had reasons for withholding Ellis' existence, but that didn't make it right.

I wonder how this will affect Ellis once he finds out the truth of what I did. Will he hate me?

Kenneth reacted to the news with threats, and I thought jealousy fueled him because he's an ass. But maybe, deep down, he's hurt too. He could've found me long ago if he wanted to, but he didn't. It was his son that evoked him to come here. He only wants me to inflict punishment. I'm sure of it.

"Soph, I didn't mean…. That look on your face is why I didn't want to say anything." Owen reaches over and takes my hand. "You did the right thing. I know Kenneth is Ellis' father, but he doesn't deserve your sympathy or your thoughts."

"It was right for me, but what about Ellis? What will he think?"

"He won't think. He will know that you are the best mom in the world because you've never given him a reason to doubt it."

I turn back to Owen, and he's staring at me as if I could never do wrong. I force a tight-lipped smile, praying that he's right. "Do you think you'll ever move past your parents' discretions?"

"Already working on it." Owen winks and flashes a sad smile.

"And Bonnie, do you see a relationship there in the future?"

"Maybe after getting on track with my parents. Bonnie is a pretty decent lady, and I have a brother who's not so bad either." Owen chuckles. "He doesn't think the world of me at the moment, but maybe in time. So, it's worth keeping the line of contact open for sure."

"Your heart is still as big as the day we met." I stare at Owen in awe, wondering how he continues to look at me the same.

The rest of the ride to Dalton's house is quiet, with both of us in our thoughts. Joselyn greets us at the door when we arrive, and Dalton appears a few seconds later.

I assume the boys are occupied since they are nowhere to be found.

"Do you mind if I steal Sophia away for a bit?" Joselyn asks Owen—like I'm not capable of deciding for myself.

Owen is still by my side with his palm resting at the base of my spine on my back. He looks at me, and I nod. "Yeah, but don't make the conversation all about me this time," he jokes.

"Pssh. What have you done to Owen?" Joselyn asks me. "You're really feeling yourself now. You used to be the most subtle," she tells Owen.

"Hey." Owen and Dalton object simultaneously.

"I'm still subtle," Owen chuckles.

"I can be subtle." Dalton laughs.

Joselyn's eyebrows rise as she focuses on Dalton. He gives her a look that's easily deciphered, and she clears her throat and looks away.

Owen kisses the side of my head. "I'll fill Dalton in if you don't mind."

"Not at all."

"Let's go." Joselyn drags me away without replying to Dalton.

Joselyn and I settle on the high stools at the bar in the kitchen.

"It's been a while since we've had a chance to talk. That Kenneth character appeared, and you went poof." Joselyn rests her elbow on the countertop.

"I know. I've felt removed from my life since Kenneth found me, and with Owen and I splitting up, it's been a hard month."

"Wait. What?" Joselyn's eyes widen as she slaps the marble beneath her palm.

I closed my mouth at her reaction. I had forgotten that I hadn't told her or Dalton my whole story. They don't know about my abusive past or my brief separation from Owen.

"I should probably fill you in." I mirror Joselyn's position, setting my arm on the counter opposite hers. A funnel of air oozes from my mouth before I begin to spill my secrets.

Joselyn's mouth hangs open the entire time, and she clings to every word I say, her expressions a mix of shock, anger, and sympathy.

I look away from her when I'm done, understanding each emotion she portrayed, but I dislike the latter because I'm not sure I deserve it.

"Hey, fix your face." Joselyn places her hand on top of mine on the counter, drawing my eyes back to her. "It wasn't your fault."

"I know. It's just hard to accept."

"This explains a lot."

"How so?"

"Owen was not himself on tour. There was a sadness about him that he tried to hide, but I noticed. He was lost without you, and that means a lot. He's not one to get lost. He cares about you." Joselyn smiles.

"I only wanted to keep him safe."

"A piece of advice?" Joselyn asks, and I nod. "This band of brothers that we're tied to do not shy away from anything. Whatever you're feeling, let Owen in. Whatever obstacles you face, face them together. He wouldn't want it any other way." She gives my hand a comforting squeeze. "And if anything else comes up that requires a woman's perspective, I'm your girl." She winks. "We're family, and we're friends."

I smile. "Thank you."

A loud noise sounds, gaining our attention. We react immediately, hurrying in that direction. We stop at the entrance to the living room, gasping at the same time when we find the source.

Twenty-Six

Owen

Sophia shouts through the living room, "Dalton!" Her chest is heaving and eyes frantic as she glares at him.

I'm just as surprised as she is. One minute we're standing next to the sliding glass door talking, and the next, Dalton has me pinned against it. His forearm is shoved onto my neck as if he wants to choke the life out of me. My hands are raised beside my head, refusing to react to his frustration.

I just filled Dalton in on what happened. I could see the anger building in him as I spoke, but I didn't expect it to be directed at me. I can only imagine what he's thinking. To me, I was respecting Sophia's wishes when I left. But to Dalton, I broke my word. I told him that I would protect her, and I failed. And even though he knew about our breakup, he didn't know why. He didn't know about Sophia's background.

Dalton jerks his head in Sophia's direction. "He left you with that piece of...."

"Dalton," Joselyn speaks up before he can get the word out and walks further inside the room. "The important thing is he's here now." Her eyes darted to me for a second before moving back to Dalton. She places her hand on his arm when she reaches him, and he seems to relax, releasing some of the pressure on my neck, but he doesn't immediately let go.

Sophia comes closer, still fuming, and forces Dalton's arm away from me. "Let go of him. Owen is not to blame here." Sophia steps between us with her back to me.

If everyone weren't so serious, I would take a moment to acknowledge how turned on I am by Sophia for coming to my aid. I didn't need her to step in—Dalton and I would've worked it out like gentlemen eventually—but fuck if it's not hot.

My hands instinctively fall to Sophia's hips. She covers my left hand with hers, calming my temper, but inciting a need for her at the same time.

"What were you thinking?" She berates Dalton. "You've known Owen a lot longer than you've known me."

"But you're my sister," Dalton says, eyeing us both.

"Yes, but I'm not your nor Owen's responsibility. *I* decide for myself. Owen only did what I asked, and as you can see, he's just as stubborn as you are. He didn't give up. He gave me the space I needed, but he's here now. If you want to be angry with someone, be angry with me."

"But you didn't do anything wrong." Dalton's features soften.

"And neither did Owen. You should apologize." Sophia tilts her head slightly to the side and folds her arms over her chest.

I can't help but chuckle behind her.

Dalton tries to hold his amusement inside but fails, his lips turning up on one side.

Sophia clears her throat, waiting, and Joselyn laughs too.

"I'm sorry," Dalton says.

"Good." Sophia moves from between us. "Now hug it out." She points at both of us, leaving no room for discussion, no alternate choice to be made.

Dalton and I engage in a quick brotherly embrace, then part with a cool handshake. His chest is a little less puffed when he steps back, but I can tell he's still not over it.

"What happens now?" Dalton rubs his hand down his cheek.

"Owen's father agreed to help. Don't worry. Ellis and I will be okay."

"You need better security. Maybe you should stay here for a while." Dalton's suggestion has all eyes on him.

"I am not running from this. I won't let Kenneth force Ellis and me out of our home." Sophia stands her ground, refusing Dalton's offer.

"I'll stay with them," I assure Dalton. He squints his eyes as if he doesn't believe I can keep them safe. I don't think he understands the lengths I would endure for them.

Dalton returns his attention to Sophia without acknowledging my statement. "If you need anything."

"I have Owen," Sophia says, glancing my way. "He's more than capable of taking care of all of my needs." She drags her finger under my chin.

Joselyn laughs.

Dalton runs a hand down his face. "I wish I could unhear that."

I want to hear it again.

I grab Sophia's hand, pulling her close. "Don't worry." I look Dalton straight in his eyes. "They're my family too."

Dalton stares at me for a long moment before nodding. "Anything," he says to me.

"Owen!" A small, loud voice comes from the entrance, and our heads turn in that direction. Ellis comes barreling toward me, much like the last time I saw him. His arms wrap around me, and I hug him back.

"Hey, Bud." I'm just as excited to see him as he is me. I didn't think I'd get the chance again. I admit to being jealous of Kenneth's time with Ellis while I was away. I know that Kenneth is his father, but Ellis is my son in every way that counts. "I missed you."

"Are you coming home?" Ellis' hopeful eyes watch me, and so does everyone else.

Joselyn has her hand over her heart as she sighs, "Oh, how sweet."

How do I say no to that?

The fact that he wants me to share his space is heartwarming. And even though it's not my home, I missed it as if it were. I can't say no. "Yeah. I'm coming home."

I missed this—Sophia, Ellis, and I relaxing on the couch watching movies. I can't help the smile that creeps onto my face as I watch them. Ellis is sitting between us, and my arm is stretched behind their heads over the top of the couch. They are totally invested in the movie that's playing, but I'm invested in them.

It's a school night and almost eleven PM, but Sophia agreed to let Ellis stay up past his bedtime just for tonight.

Ellis yawns and stretches as the movie credits begin to roll. He lays his head on Sophia's shoulder briefly before straightening again.

Sophia and I grin at how tired he is, but he doesn't want to admit it.

"Alright, Bud. It's time for bed. I won't have the school calling me because you fell asleep in class." Sophia nudges Ellis forward until he stands.

"But I want to stay with Owen," Ellis complains.

The sadness in his eyes breaks my heart because I know it has everything to do with me. He's afraid that I'm going to leave again.

Sophia glances my way, and I surmise that she's thinking the same thing.

I can't promise that I won't go away again, but I can assure him that I'll be here when he wakes up in the morning.

"Tell you what," I say to Ellis. "Get some sleep, and I'll take you to school in the morning myself."

Ellis stares at me for a few seconds. "Deal." He smiles sleepily, yawning again. "Will you be my dad?" Ellis blurts out.

My eyes fly open. "I…." *I don't know what to say.* "You already have a father."

"I like you better," Ellis says, seriously.

Sophia snickers next to me, and I glance at her wanting to do the same, but I don't want Ellis to think I'm laughing at him. So, I conceal my amusement and concentrate on the importance of the moment.

I clear my throat, focusing on Ellis. "If it were up to me, I'd say yes. I would love nothing more than to be your dad, but it's not up to me."

"Well, who is it up to?" Ellis tilts his head to the side, staring me down.

Kids. They ask the hardest questions and tell you exactly what they want because to them; everything is simple. It's yes or no. This or that. There is no in-between.

I look at Sophia, and her smile sobers. She grabs Ellis' hand. "That would be you and me, Bud."

I like that Sophia doesn't include Kenneth in the decision because he doesn't deserve a say. My heart swells, but I remain stoic.

"Do you want him to be my dad?" Ellis asks Sophia.

Sophia smiles widely. "I would like that very much."

"Are you going to live with us?" Ellis turns to me.

"Okay, that's enough questions for tonight," Sophia cuts in. "Bed. Now, Little Mister." She points toward the hallway.

This time I grin. I can't believe how much I love this kid.

Ellis follows Sophia's instructions walking away from us. His sleep-filled voice sounds over his shoulder as he moves. "Good night, Mom. Good night, Dad."

Ellis disappears, but his words repeat inside my head.

Dad.

The title suits me, bringing a huge smile to my face.

I turn to Sophia and open my arm for her to come closer. She swings her legs across my thighs, sitting sideways, and her arms go around my neck.

"Dad, huh?" She teases, but I'm okay with that. I meant what I said.

"You sure you're okay with that?" I touch my forehead to hers.

"I'm more than okay. It wouldn't be a bad idea if you spent your nights and days here either." Sophia's fingers tease the hair at the base of my neck.

My arms go around her, pulling her fully onto my lap. "Are you asking me to move in with you, Soph?"

"I'm saying that if or when you're ready, the option is on the table."

"I'm all for it, on one condition." I kiss the tip of her nose.

"What's that?" Sophia tilts her head to look into my eyes.

"Promise me you'll never push me away again."

"I promise." She presses her lips to mine, and I kiss her, slow and steady.

Twenty-Seven

Sophia

Maggie follows me into my office the next morning. "What cloud are *you* on today?"

I plop down into my chair, and a gush of air flows out of me. Lately, I've been floating somewhere between one and five, but today is different. Even though I still have to deal with Kenneth, I have Owen back in my life. So, my peak has gotten substantially higher.

"Cloud ten, Maggie. Cloud ten." I sigh.

"So, I take it that things went well after you left." Maggie stops in front of my desk.

"Better than well." I sit forward, gazing at her. "I want to thank you for what you did."

Maggie waves my comment away. "I didn't do anything but tell a teensy white lie," she grins. "But it was for a good cause."

"Yes, it was."

Maggie sets a folder on my desk in front of me. "Now, here is your first client of the day. They should be arriving in a few minutes."

I open the file, skimming through it. "You may bring them back when they arrive."

"Sure thing." Maggie turns to leave but stops at the door to look back at me. "I'm glad it worked out," she says, sincerely. Then, she's gone.

"Me too," I whispered.

My clients arrive right on time, and I go through the motions as I've done so many times, except I've never been this high on life. When they leave, I'm still in the sky. I don't think anything can bring me down today.

They were my only clients before lunch. So, I called the security company once they left to beef up my protection at home to keep Kenneth from dropping by when he felt like it—something I should've done after the first occurrence.

Maggie knocks on my door right before lunch, and I wave her inside. Her smile is all teeth when she enters, and her cheeks are flushed. "You have a visitor," she sings.

"Is this another one of your teensy white lies?" I eye her curiously.

"Nope. Owen is here to see you. And he brought a guest."

I bunch my brows in confusion. "A guest."

Maggie nods. "And a fine one at that."

"Send them in."

I stand, looking myself over, and brushing my hands down the front of my dress, at the same time, wondering who the guest could be.

Owen turns the corner first, donned in blue jeans and a solid black t-shirt, and my cloud level rises with each step he takes toward me.

A guy, who appears to be in his thirties, follows Owen inside. He's wearing all-black pants and a black button-up with a long black tie. He stops just inside the door, tall, brooding, and holds his left wrist with his right hand as if he's on assignment. He has a terrifying look about him, which I recognize from experience.

Maggie is beside herself, her eyes burning a hole into him. "I'll be right outside if you need me," she says to me but still focused on the guy by the door.

The door closes, and Owen reaches me, placing a kiss on my temple. "Hey."

"Hey. New security detail?" I ask.

"Yeah. That's Chance. Your new bodyguard." Owen grabs my hand, guiding me around the desk and walking over to him. "Chance, meet my future wife, Sophia. Sophia, meet Chance."

"Nice to meet you, Ma'am," Chance nods, his voice stern.

"And you as well." I pause for a second. More than a few thoughts run through my head, but I can only focus on one at a time. "Chance, would you mind giving Owen and me a moment?"

"Not at all, Ma'am." Chance opens the door and steps outside my office door, closing it behind him.

I pull Owen away from the door and turn to face him. "A bodyguard? I don't need a bodyguard, Owen."

Owen places his hands on the sides of my arms. "Just let me do this, okay. I can't always be with you, Soph. There will be days, sometimes weeks, that I'm away. I need to know that you and Ellis are safe. It's the only way I know how to do that. It's the only way I can do my job without feeling guilty about leaving."

"I guess you're right," I say after a long moment. And with the Kenneth situation unresolved, it couldn't hurt.

Owen's hands massage my arms before settling on my hips. He pulls me flush against him. "You won't even know he's there."

"Are you sure about that? Because I'm sure that *everyone* knows that he's there. Maggie wanted to jump the poor guy's bones. Aren't you worried that I might get attached?" I grin.

Owen smirks, bringing his hand to my cheek and brushing his thumb over it. "No, you only have eyes for me," he says with so much confidence that even I believe him. "And I only have eyes for you. No one comes between us."

His hand cups the back of my head, and he pressed his lips to mine, kissing me deeply.

My body reacts to him, warming, teasing, wanting more of him. I force our lips apart, breathing heavily. "We have to stop," I admit grudgingly.

Owen's lips turn up in a dangerous smirk. "Or we could lock the door and turn down the blinds. There are a few things I'd like to do to you on that desk." His thumb moves across my lips, and a throbbing sensation hits me down below.

I swallow my excitement, ignoring the need to take him up on his offer. I open my mouth to respond and close it just as quickly when my office door flies open.

Maggie comes rushing inside, her eyes frantic. "Excuse me for interrupting, but that guy. Mr. Weatherby is back and demanding to see you. Chance," Maggie says, and I raise my brow, wondering when they became acquainted. "The guard has him contained, but he's not happy."

Owen turns, looking from Maggie to me. "Mr. Weatherby?"

"Kenneth. It's how he introduced himself when he showed up," I explained. Maggie never knew his real name, and I guess she doesn't follow the news either. I failed to mention it to Owen as well.

That's all Owen needed to hear. He moves so quickly, and I go after him, but it's impossible to stop him. Chance is blocking Kenneth by the door, and Owen reaches them in seconds. Both Kenneth and Owen sport looks that could kill, and everyone in the office has a front-row seat to the action.

I could care less about Kenneth. He shouldn't have come here. Owen is my only concern.

"Maggie, call the police," I say with urgency.

Owen tries to get his hands on Kenneth, but Chance blocks him, lifting his arm in front of Owen. "Let me handle this, Sir," Chance says, keeping his focus on Kenneth.

I step in front of Owen, place my palms to his chest, and attempt to move him back, but I barely make a dent in his stance. He stumbles back a fraction as his heart beats furiously against my hands.

"Owen." I touch the sides of his face. "Owen, look at me." His fists are clenched, chest profound, and eyes like daggers until they find mine. "He's not worth it."

"Did you forget what we discussed, Jo?" Kenneth's voice booms behind me. "You're mine or no one's."

"She's not your fucking possession," Owen seethes, his gaze flicking back to Kenneth.

I drop my hands, turning to face Kenneth, trying to remain composed, and Owen wraps his arms protectively around my waist.

"I am not your property, Kenneth, and I won't let you threaten the people I love or me anymore. If you want a relationship with your son, it's yours, but that's as far as *we* go."

Kenneth's eyes are like fire, scorching every part of me they touch. He's quiet for a long moment. Then, he jerks away from Chance. A menacing grin bubbles out of him as he stares at me.

Chance still has his arms up, but his shoulders relax a bit. "Are you okay?" he glances over his shoulder at me.

"Yes." I nod, and in the next breath, Kenneth grabs me. His hand goes around my neck, squeezing, taking my breath away. I don't have time to think. My eyes widen at the unexpected pain that shoots through me, the sudden loss of air that quiets me.

An alarm screeches inside my head, and I grab Kenneth's wrist, tugging to no avail.

"Ggg…." I tried to speak, but a low gurgle was all I could manage.

Worried, muffled voices ring out around me, rapidly fading into the background.

The warmth of Owen's arms evaporates, and my knees weaken. It's a wonder how I'm still standing.

A memory flashes inside my head, making it hard to distinguish the past from the present.

My arm goes limp.

Chance moves.

I see Owen in front of me.

I don't see Kenneth.

My breath returns with a harsh rush. My body bends at the waist as I grab my neck, coughing, still a little dazed.

The voices are hushed now but more distinct.

The warmth comes back, and I lean back onto a hard, familiar body.

Owen.

I glance toward the exit where Chance has regained control over Kenneth. His hands are secured behind his back with a zip tie. His proud smirk is aimed straight at me.

A siren sounds in the distance, getting closer by the second. A few moments later, flashing lights come into view, stopping directly in front of the entrance.

"You're a lying, thieving bitch," Kenneth says, too calmly.

"Let's go," Chance opens the door to escort Kenneth outside.

Kenneth gave me a final glance, declaring, "This isn't over."

I turn into Owen's arms once Kenneth is out of sight, burying my face in his chest. How do I face my co-workers after that fiasco?

"You're safe now. He's gone. We'll fix this." Owen encourages, kissing the side of my head and wrapping his arms around me. He holds me for a few seconds, then pulls back to look at me. "Soph, we need to speak with the cops."

It's not the first time I've been given the option to tell my truth about Kenneth, but it is the first time that I'm not willing to tell a lie. He deserves to be punished for what he did, for what he's still threatening to do.

"I'm ready." I unconsciously touch my neck, the vile sting of Kenneth's grip still palpable. I turn to face everyone in the office, and that look of sympathy is so potent on their faces that I feel as if it's smothering me. It's quiet, yet so loud. Their eyes tell me exactly what they want me to know, and I want to run and hide from every one of their tells, but I hold my head high instead, taking normal painful steps with Owen by my side until the sun hits my face.

Twenty-Eight

Owen

I wanted to kill Kenneth. I wanted to wrap my hands around his neck, as he had done to Sophia, and choke the life out of him. The only obstacle keeping me from doing so was Sophia. My fear for her stopped me. I had to know that she was okay.

It's been three weeks since Kenneth was hauled away by the cops. Sophia pressed charges this time and had no issues proving her claim. Cell phone footage was everywhere, from every angle, detailing what happened from the moment Kenneth barged into Sophia's office making demands. He was charged with assault and battery, ordered to serve twenty days in jail, and given thirty days of probation once he got out.

It's not nearly enough for what Sophia has endured at the hands of him, but something good came out of all the bad. My dad worked his magic. Kenneth will never have custody of Ellis. Because of his charges, it's up to Sophia if she wants Ellis to see Kenneth again, and even then, visits would have to be supervised. He's prohibited from making direct contact with Sophia, verbal or otherwise, due to the restraining order.

Even with that document signed into law, I can't seem to let my guard down. Kenneth is a wild card that is one day fresh out of jail, and I keep playing his last words on repeat in my head.

This isn't over.

Warmth covers my hand resting on the cool leather between us in the back seat of my truck. "What's on your mind?" Sophia asks the sunlight accenting her beautiful smile.

I glance over, returning her smile. "I'm thinking about how cute you are." I lift her hand to my lips, placing a kiss on the back of it, then settling on my lap.

"Just cute?" Sophia teases.

"Not just cute, but strong. I adore you, Soph."

I glanced at Ellis, passed out in the rear seat behind us, then returned my attention to Sophia. The partition is down. Frank is driving with Chance in the passenger seat, and they're both pretending again like they don't hear a thing.

"And I cherish you, Owen."

I can't tell Sophia that I'm not as cool and calm as I look when she's so excited about me meeting her mother. The closer we get to enemy territory, the more alert my senses become.

"My mom is going to love you," Sophia says.

"Is that code for, get ready to be drilled?" I chuckle.

"Maybe. Maybe not." Sophia faces forward.

A few minutes later, the smile drops from Sophia's face. Her whole demeanor changes until we turn at the stoplight leading to her mom's house. Pindrop silence fills the air for the remainder of the drive. Relief showers her when she steps inside her mom's house with Ellis and me behind her.

Ellis runs straight for Jinx, the dog that Sophia mentioned a few days ago, and her mom watches him with an amused shake of her head before focusing on me.

Sophia and I talked about meeting her mom days ago. She said she was hesitant to bring it up because of her stepmom, Ruth, and how close I am to her. I explained to her that the past is the past, and regardless of how close I am with Ruth, I won't let that dictate the future that Sophia and I have. If her mother is important to her, then she's important to me.

"Owen." Jillian, Sophia's mom, says my name as if she already knows me, and I wonder what information she's privy to. "Nice to finally meet you. I've heard nothing but good things."

"Nice to meet you, Miss…."

"Jillian. Just Jillian," she says, stepping close to me. "Thank you for being there for my baby." She wraps her arms around me, pinning my arms by my sides.

I freeze, shocked by her action, but glad she approves. I had no qualms about meeting Sophia's mother. I'm good with people, but I wasn't expecting a hug at first sight.

Jillian releases me and steps back.

"I appreciate that, but I don't deserve the credit. Sophia does. She was strong for both of us, even when I had no clue she needed to be." Sophia put herself at risk to protect me. If that's not evidence of her love for me, I don't know what is. I glance at Sophia for a moment, then turn back. "Thank you for trusting me with Sophia."

Jillian brings her hand to rest over her heart, shifting her eyes to Sophia. "Where did you find him again?"

Sophia giggles. "I didn't. *He* rescued me." She grabs my hand, squeezing gently. She looks up at me. Her eyes seem to sparkle, and she blushes.

Every part of me takes notice. I drop my eyes to Sophia's lips, and she licks them. I want to kiss them. I clear my throat, not wanting but needing to look away, thinking, *not in front of her mother.*

"Okay," Jillian draws out. "Let's get you, kids, something cold to drink." She turns and begins walking away.

Sophia and I let out a quiet laugh, not embarrassed in the least.

The day flew by unnoticeably between Ellis and Jinx running around and Jillian going to and from the kitchen. Jillian asked me tons of questions—nothing too invasive—and I answered all of them, even the one about my intentions with Sophia. I've never hidden the fact that I want forever with Sophia. So, when Jillian asked, I told her as much.

And she rewarded me heavily.

"You didn't have to go to all this trouble, Jillian." I stare down at the healthy plate of food in front of me on the table—brown rice, mac and cheese, green beans, and smothered chops. Then, I glance at the lemon cake at the center.

"Nonsense. Now eat up." Jillian looks around the table, pausing at each set of eyes. Somehow, she managed to talk Frank and Chance into taking a break to eat with us, and they appear all kinds of awkward.

Sophia knocks my knee with hers under the table. "You heard the woman. Eat up," she says, wiggling her brows.

All of us dive in, and when I'm done, I can hardly breathe because I'm stuffed. Sophia and I volunteer to wash the dishes afterward while everyone else is outside. I stare out of the kitchen window into the backyard, snickering under my breath. Even Frank and Chance have loosened up. Maybe they're like me and need to burn off some of the weight of our meal.

"You seem content," Sophia says next to me with her hands paused under the water flowing into the sink. She pulls the last plate from the sink, rinsing it, and places it on the drying mat beside her.

"Because I am." I dip my finger in the sudsy water and tap her nose.

"Hey," Sophia protests, and I wrap my arms around her waist, pulling her close.

"Finally, a free moment alone." I press my lips to hers, and she lets out an audible moan. Her hands grip the shirt at my sides as she leans into me. My lips move to her neck, and my tongue snakes out, sucking softly.

A throat clears behind us, and Sophia goes still. I jerk my head up and turn around to find Jillian watching us.

"You two keep that up, and I'll have to douse you." Jillian grins. "Oh, the joys of being young and in love." Jillian walks further inside, sniffing the air.

"Everything okay, Mom?" Sophia watches her intently.

"It smelled like smoke outside, so I came in to ask you the same thing." Jillian turns the corner, disappearing behind the wall leading to the living room, and we follow behind her. She opens the door and gasps. We stop short, peering outside into the front yard.

"No," Sophia says, her hand grasping for something to hold on to.

Kenneth is standing in the front yard staring at the house. Close to the front porch, a small fire burns a few feet away from him. He doesn't seem surprised to see us or phased by our sudden appearance. A tall bottle is in one hand and a lighter in the other. He lights the cloth hanging from the bottle targeting his sinister gaze at us. He doesn't try to hide his disdain. He wanted us to witness this moment.

"No," Sophia says again, backing up slowly.

Jillian doesn't move. I'm not sure if she's in shock or enraged because I can't see her face. "Get off of my property!" She yells, answering my unspoken question. She takes two steps, and I grab her arm to stop her.

"Jillian, don't," I pleaded. Kenneth is obviously out of his mind. He doesn't seem to care about the consequences.

"Mom?" I hear Ellis' questioning voice from somewhere outside.

Kenneth looks away for a split second before returning his gaze to us. "You can't protect them all," he says above the crackle of the fire between us.

"Ellis!" Sophia shouts, attempting to go around Jillian and me, but it's too late.

Kenneth raises his hand above his head, and with a baleful glare, he releases the bottle, tossing it in our direction. At the same time, he's knocked off of his feet as Chance rams into his side. They hit the ground hard, and the bottle lands just shy of the porch.

"Mom," Ellis says frantically.

Sophia moves so fast that I barely recognize her, and she reaches Ellis instantly. Her arms are tight around him by the time I catch up. I wrap my arms around both of them, letting out a breath of relief.

Jillian calls the cops, and they arrive within minutes.

Kenneth doesn't fight when the handcuffs are clamped around his wrist. There's no remorse in his eyes, only pure hatred. I wonder what could possess a man or anyone to behave the way he has.

Sophia instructed Ellis to wait inside with Jillian while she and I stood on the front porch as Kenneth settled into the back of the police car.

I hold her hand beside me as she looks on with an unreadable expression.

"What are you thinking?" I ask.

"I'm thinking that Chance is totally worth the loss of privacy." Sophia looks at me. "If he hadn't…." Her voice trails off, but I know precisely what she meant. Kenneth's actions could've seriously hurt someone.

I wrap my arm around her waist, pulling her to my side. "It's over now." I press my lips to her temple, remaining there for a few seconds before pulling away.

Kenneth is hauled off once again, and I've never been more grateful because this time, he's going to get what he deserves.

UNSUNG MELODIES

Epilogue

Six Months Later

Owen

Being away from Sophia and Ellis still hasn't gotten any easier, but at least now, my mind is at ease knowing that Kenneth is behind bars where he belongs. He suffered a harsh punishment for attempting to set fire to Jillian's home and endangering our lives. Ellis will be a grown man by the time he's even eligible for parole.

The guys and I have been home for a couple of weeks now, and I've spent every moment making up for the time I was away.

Today is special because it's a first for all of us. The owner of Melodies allowed us to rent the place out for the night, and all of our families were invited to watch us perform live at the place where it all started. After talking it over with my parents first, I even invited Bonnie and Donald—not that I needed their approval. I only wanted them to be aware.

Bonnie and I have a great relationship now, and I think Donald has a lot to do with that. If he hadn't reached out to me months ago, I would've stayed away. I didn't want to force my presence on him until he was ready. We've hung out a few times, just Donald and me, and we seem to be moving in the right direction. He's not angry with me anymore. So, that's a plus.

Jillian and Ruth seem to be getting along well too. Weirdly, they have this twisted bond because of Sophia's father, because of us. I guess sometimes time does heal wounds. Its measure gives minds the will to change and the strength to forgive the unforgivable.

"Dad, how much longer are you going to be?" Ellis walks up to me, looking bored, and I chuckle.

"Not much longer, Bud."

Sophia ruffles his hair. "Be patient. Go join your cousins." She nudges him toward the corner where Luke's nephews and Dalton's son are seated. Then she turns to me. "Are you ready for this?"

"I was born for this," I tell her, placing a kiss on her forehead.

Sophia looks into my eyes. "Did you ever think we'd end up here before we started dating?"

Our fingers intertwined by our sides.

"I didn't know the time or the place, but I knew that I would end up with you. Since the moment I saw you, I have wanted you in my life. And since I always get what I want, eventually, I knew that you would be my someone at some point in time."

"Such a wise man."

"This wise man has been thinking." I wiggle my brows.

"Nope." Rose interrupts. "None of that in front of the kids." She jokes.

"We're stealing her away now," Joselyn says, looping her arm through Sophia's and successfully disconnecting our fingers. "The guys are ready for you."

Rose directs me to turn, then gives me a subtle push toward the manager's office. "Go. There will be time for play later."

I laugh on my way to the office, and the guys are, in fact, waiting on me.

"Your wives are something else," I tell them, and they chuckle.

"Yeah," Luke agrees. "Hard to believe we're family men now."

"We've come a long way for sure," Dalton says, massaging his chin between his fingers. "And that crowd out there is proof of it. My mom is friends with Jillian," he says, unbelieving. "My father would be pissed if he were alive to see this day."

"I never thought I'd be comfortable in the same room with my brother and his wife after what they did to me, but here we are," Luke adds.

"Yeah," I sigh happily. "Here we are—a ready-made family, a dad, two moms, a brother, a host of extended family, and two of the best friends a guy could ask for."

"I think that's enough," Luke stands up. "You just made it weird."

"How?" I grin.

"By making it sound like a funeral pamphlet," Luke answers.

Dalton stands too. "Let's go give them the show they've been waiting for."

Ten minutes later, we're on a makeshift stage with our gear performing for our family as if they were strangers in the crowd, except their cheers resonate on a deeper level. It makes my heart swell. I never thought I'd see the day when my parents watched me on stage with so much pride in their eyes, free of fear and disappointment.

Dalton quiets everyone down when we get to the final song, as he always does when we perform. He thanks everyone for coming out and tells everyone how much we love them. Then, calls Sophia to the stage to stand next to him. He puts his arm around her shoulder, facing the crowd, and begins talking, but I tune him out because my next move is all I can think of.

I walk up behind Sophia while Dalton has her attention, and I get down on one knee. I pull the ring I'd bought when I returned from my pocket and wait for her to turn around.

Gasps fill the restaurant, but I remain focused on Sophia. When she turns around, she sucks in a breath, and her hands fly up to her mouth.

"Owen," she says, muffled beneath the cover of her hands. "What's happening?"

"This ring has been burning a hole in my pocket," I begin, "but tonight, I hope to be rid of the torture. I've never known a love like ours, Soph, and I never want to move past it. I want to grow in it, with you, with Ellis. I want to be the husband you deserve; the father Ellis needs. I love you now and forever. You're the only woman who could bring me to my knees."

I reach up and grab her hand, bringing it down to my level, and it trembles within my grasp.

"Sophia Jolene Conley, will you marry me?"

Sophia nods, her *yes* spoken hoarsely as her eyes fill with tears. "Yes," she says louder.

I slip the ring onto her finger and stand, cupping the sides of her face in my palms, and kiss her, not caring about all the eyes watching. Disregarding Dalton's request to not have to witness the action again.

I ease away from her lips, our foreheads touching, my hands traveling the length of her arms down to her hands.

My thumb skims the new addition, bringing a smile to my face.

Hands clap and voices whistle, but there's only Sophia and me at this moment.

"I love you, Owen Daye."

"I love you back. You'll always be the cutest being in the room, Soph. You'll always be my Melody."

Our bodies are jolted and attention captured by the force of Ellis throwing his arms around us. "Does this mean you can adopt me now?"

I look down into Ellis' innocent eyes, caught off guard once again.

I moved in with Sophia four months ago, after the dust with Kenneth had settled. We sat Ellis down and explained everything to him in a way that he could understand, and he was obviously paying very close attention.

Sophia wraps an arm around Ellis, including him in our bubble, and I cover her arm with mine.

"Soon, Bud. Soon."

My eyes turn warm and damp as I'm overwhelmed with emotion. One tear slips from the corner of my left eye, another from the right, and I let them fall freely. I refuse to dim this moment by hiding my true feelings.

I'm glad that our family is here to bear witness. I don't know what I did to deserve Sophia and Ellis or anyone in my presence, but I plan to do everything I can to keep them all in my life.

The End.

UNSUNG MELODIES

Acknowledgments

To My Family,
You already know, but I'll say it again. Thank you, a million times over, for your support and unconditional love.

To Mary Meredith,
The absolute best beta reader and virtual friend. It's always a pleasure. Thank you.

To Ebony McMillan,
There are no words to describe your generosity, your willingness to push forward for others at one of the most difficult points in your life. You are a rock star. Thank you.

To My Group, Parker's Angels
My safe place. Some of my biggest supporters. Huge hugs to all of you.

As Always, to all of the bloggers, authors, and everyone who had anything to do with this book's release, I thank you from the bottom of my heart. My words exist in the hands and hearts of many because of you.

Author's Note

Wow. Where Do I Begin?

I had no idea of the route this series would take me when I started writing it. I knew it would be an experience, but it turned out to be an experience that I'll never forget. There are so many ups and downs with DOL, so many moments that I already miss. They made me laugh when I was sad, cry when I was happy. These characters were my outlet, and I've enjoyed bringing their stories to life.

Now that we have all three, here's a little about their names. I put a lot of thought into who they would be as a whole before I ever wrote the first word, and I landed on 'Forever and a Day'—Dalton Evers, Lucas Anders, and Owen Daye. Though they may not make sense at first glance—each title is crafted from their profession and knitted into the fabric of their lives.

I hope that you'll fall in love with this group of rock stars as I've done and feel every emotion as I've felt them. I hope to be another star in your eyes very soon.

As always in parting...

Everything that anyone does, big or small, plays a huge part in an author's success. I appreciate you all so very much. Thanks for coming along with me on my journey. If you enjoyed reading my book, please consider posting a review on your preferred site, and don't forget to tell your friends about me.

Until Next Time...

About the Author

Angela K. Parker is a country girl with a big heart. She's a South Carolina native with a passion for writing, reading, music, & math. When she's not engaged in any of the above, she's spending time with her family or catching up on the latest movies. She's always had a very active imagination. Now she's putting it to good use.

Connect With the Author

Visit www.angelakparker.com and sign up for Angela's newsletter to be informed of future releases.

Email: angelaparkerauthor@gmail.com

Printed in Great Britain
by Amazon